Night Dreams and Night Screams

Lawrence Falcetano

Night Dreams and Night Screams
Copyright © 2020 Lawrence Falcetano

All rights reserved. No part of this publication may be reproduced, distributed, or transmitted in any form or by any means, including photocopying, recording, or other electronic or mechanical methods without prior written permission from the author.

This is a work of fiction. Names, characters, businesses, places, events and incidents are either the product of the author's imagination or used in a fictitious manner. Any resemblance to actual persons, living or dead, or actual events is purely coincidental.

First Edition

Dedication:

The stories in this collection are dedicated to my wife, who courageously read each one.

"You can come out from under the bed now."

CONTENTS:

Mr. Reaper 1
Night Work 16
Silent, Secret 24
Cassie 31
Easy Take 37
The Collectors 45
Red Rose, Dead Rose 49
Beware, The Willow Wood! 57
Ridley's Rat 65
The Callings 81
The Men of Salem County 90
Morena's Revenge 93
Dark Places 102
The Thing in The Closet 111
The Devil's Details 119
The Visitation 130
The Secret of Skinny Bigelow 140
Welcome to The Doll House 149
The Man in The Wall 162

Mr. Reaper

"You never want to die?" the man said.

"No, I never want to be killed. There's a difference."

"Of course," the man said. "But why would you make such a request?"

"Can you make it happen?"

"Certainly," the man said with an air of arrogance. "But you haven't answered my question."

Walter Culpepper adjusted his rimless glasses and leaned his slender frame across the table to get a better look at the stranger sitting before him. The man was impeccably dressed in a black suit, white shirt, and a black cravat tie. A white gardenia was pinned delicately in his left lapel. White linen gloves covered his hands. His shiny black hair was combed back tight against his head and contrasted with his sallow skin and pale deep-set eyes. Walter reached out and gingerly poked the man's shoulder with his finger. "Are you real?" he said.

"As real as you want me to be," the man said.

"How did you get in here?"

"You called for me. I'm Mr. Reaper."

"I didn't call for you," Walter said. "And I don't know anyone named, Reaper."

"But you did," the man said. "You willed me here through your thoughts, your desire to make changes in your life. I am here to help you."

"Are you an angel?"

"Hardly," the man said with a smile that held a hint of amusement.

"This is crazy. How did you get in my house?"

"I told you I was summoned. If, however, you have changed your mind, I have a full schedule and perhaps someone else may be of service to you."

The man stood and pushed his chair back to leave, but Walter stopped him with, "What kind of service do you offer?"

Mr. Reaper took his seat again, rested his gloved hands on the table, laced his fingers together and said, "Tell me what your needs are...precisely."

Walter sat back in his chair, took a deep breath, collected his thoughts, then warily began: "I'm sure we can both agree that most people have fears, fears that manifest themselves in many ways."

"Fear is a weakening of the human spirit," Mr. Reaper said.

"Exactly," Walter said. "It interferes with a person's life, the way one lives. But if a person could eradicate their fears, live completely fearless, one could achieve one's goals and desires without obstruction. That to me would be the ultimate way to live. Afraid of nothing. For that, I would give anything."

"An interesting philosophy, considering how short a human life is."

"All my life I've been a wimp," Walter continued, "A pathetic loser, afraid of everything outside my comfort zone. Pushed around, shouted at, laughed at and disrespected. The puny little banker who goes to work every day and comes home to the endless humiliations of an indifferent, henpecking wife."

"I see," Mr. Reaper said. "And how would you utilize this fearless existence?"

"I'd walk about the world boldly, unburdened of my past fears. I'd confront adversity with a smile, a snicker, even arrogance. I'd laugh in the face of death."

Mr. Reaper raised his eyebrows. "I wouldn't go that far," he said. "Tell me, how would our agreement be terminated? How would you like the end to come? There must be an end, even for you, to consummate the agreement."

"I want to go naturally," Walter said.

"Naturally, as in what medical science terms, 'natural causes'?"

"Yes, old age. Call it what you like."

Mr. Reaper leaned forward and folded his arms on the table. "Let's understand each other," he said. "You want to be protected from death in every way except by nature's way. You want to be immune from murder, suicide, accident, disease, manmade or natural disasters, or harm in any way. Therefore, not fearing any of the aforementioned."

"Exactly," Walter said. "I'd give you my soul for that."

Mr. Reaper leaned back in his chair again. "I don't collect souls," he said. "That's a job for someone higher up—or *down*— so to speak. I am merely the conduit, the deliverer. I make arrangements. Offer choices."

"What kind of choices?" Walter said.

"Everyone must leave this world sooner or later. Most people don't know where, how or when their time will come. I remove those uncertainties through negotiation. People take comfort in knowing the reason and time of their demise. But they must be willing to relinquish what they deem to be their most precious possession in the agreement."

"Like their soul?" Walter said.

"If it is the bargain," Mr. Reaper said.

"And our bargain will be, that I'll live a very long time, afraid of nothing, and die only of old age."

"Precisely. In your case, I can guarantee the *how* but not the *when*. When your time arrives, I will arrange for delivery to the entity I represent, that which you have willingly bartered here today."

"What entity might that be?" Walter said.

"I am constrained from full disclosure," Mr. Reaper said. "Are you afraid?"

Walter squared his shoulders in a display of feigned courage. "No," he said. "I'm not afraid and I won't be afraid." He looked boldly at Mr. Reaper and said: "Tell me how, exactly, will it happen. I mean, if by chance I should fall victim to an incident that would, under normal circumstances, end my life. How will I survive? Will there be pain? Will I realize death?"

"You will realize nothing," Mr. Reaper said. "If you should experience such an unfortunate occurrence, you will awaken as if from a short stupor. You will remember nothing about it and your life will continue. You will expire, as per our contract, only of old age. Do we have a deal, then?"

"I'm a healthy young man," Walter said, "and expect to live a very long time."

"To your advantage."

"When will it begin?"

"It already has."

"That's all there is to it?"

"Done."

"Isn't there a contract or something I need to sign?"

Mr. Reaper smiled. "You've been reading too much fiction," he said.

"Then I can't be killed or harmed in any way?"

"As you wished."

Walter sprang to his feet and let out a holler. He stretched out his arms and pounded his chest, "I've been given a new life." he said. With unbridled elation, he spun about several times on his heels. He was Superman, Hercules, a modern-day Goliath. No one could stop him now. With hardy laughter, he continued his pirouettes until he fell to the floor, caught in the whirlpool of the spinning room. When his head cleared, he looked up with a triumphant smile, but his benefactor had vanished.

Steadying himself in his seat again, Walter looked around the quiet room for some sign that what had just occurred had not been his imagination. Had it all been an illusion? Had it been a manifestation of his mind brought on by wishful thinking?

Mr. Reaper

Perhaps there was no Mr. Reaper. Perhaps he was fooling himself again, as he had done so often in the past. Maybe his insatiable desire to shed his mundane, pathetic, wife nagging life was affecting him mentally, pushing him over the edge as Doctor Markham had suggested during their last session.

His eyes scanned the familiar surroundings: his desk, (as cluttered as always), his bed, (unmade, as usual), his bedroom door, (locked), and his window, (shut tight, curtains drawn). His room was exactly as he customarily prepared it each evening before retiring for the night.

How, then, had Mr. Reaper gotten in and out?

But then he saw it, lying on the table, as delicate and innocent as a wounded butterfly, a fallen peddle from Mr. Reaper's white gardenia. Evidence it had happened. He smiled broadly to himself. Doctor Markham's prognosis of him was wrong. He had made a deal and attained the thing he wanted most—to live a long, happy life without fear. And Mr. Reaper had made it possible.

***

"Did you pick up the dry cleaning?" his wife, Mildred said.

"No," Walter said, taking his seat at the breakfast table and sampling a spoonful of nearly cold oatmeal.

"I asked you just yesterday."

"I forgot."

"You're pathetic," she said. "I asked you to do a simple thing and you can't even accomplish that. Well, you'll have to wear the only shirt you have until you get some fresh ones."

After four years of marriage, his wife's incessant nagging and complaining had reached an apex. She complained to him again and again about the same things: criticisms of their marriage, no children, no friends, and never enough money. He worked hard at the bank and although his salary was meager, it was enough for them to live comfortably. Mildred disagreed, even though she had never contributed to the marriage financially. Keeping house and picking up after him was her job, she'd said. No matter how understanding he'd tried to be, nothing satisfied her.

They had fallen in love after college and married quickly. But in time, Mildred became dissatisfied with their situation and took her frustrations out on him. Blamed him for the way they lived, for the things they didn't have. For the sake of harmony, he had tolerated it. Just as he had tolerated his superiors at the bank. Silently suffering their unwarranted humiliations because he was afraid, afraid of the negative consequences. "*Serves you right,*" Mildred was saying, "*to go to work smelling like a dirty laundry basket.*" But he didn't have to take it anymore. He wasn't afraid of Mildred, his bosses, or anyone. Today he would use his newfound courage to change his life, just as he had planned, just as he had wished. The first change he'd make would be to get rid of Mildred—permanently!

No one would miss her. With no friends or family, who would care? He'd spent recent months planning the whole thing out in his head, mindful of every detail. It was just a matter of execution, waiting for the right moment. In the past, he hadn't the courage to go through with it. But now he was devoid of fear. Tonight he would do it. While she was asleep. A pillow pressed tightly against her face was all it would take. When it was done, he would dispose of her body in the cave deep in the woods behind the house. The cave was a single cavern in the side of a hill with an entrance no wider than a man's body created by shifting earth and weather and millenniums of time. He had discovered it years ago while walking his dog. Since then the acreage of trees and undergrowth had obliterated its presence. The woods surrounding it had been abandoned for decades and there would be no way anyone would ever find her.

It amazed him how clearly he could think when he wasn't afraid.

Before attending to Mildred, he needed to take care of the business at the bank this morning With the money, and with

Mr. Reaper

Mildred out of the way, he could make his way to the West Coast and live the life he had always dreamed about.

Things were finally looking up—thanks to Mr. Reaper.

He missed his usual 7:45 bus and had to take the 8:05. That made him late for work. But today he didn't care. He wasn't afraid of what Mr. Muncie, the bank manager, would say to him. If he hadn't had things planned as he did, he would tell Muncie to "kiss-off."

Andy Holloway, the bank guard, was standing at his usual corner by the front door as Walter entered the bank. "Late again," Holloway said with a derisive smirk. "Muncie's going to be all over you."

Walter ignored the remark with a friendly smile, in the past, a uniform and a gun had always intimidated him, but now he eyed Andy Holloway as an irrelevant store manikin.

Walter went to his desk, turned on his computer and pretended to attend to the day's business. When he looked up, he saw Mr. Muncie standing in front of his desk. "You were late this morning, Culpepper," Mr. Muncie said. "That makes three times in as many weeks. Mr. Abrams won't have it much longer."

Normally, Walter would have stumbled over his words, struggling to find a plausible explanation for his tardiness, fearful of losing his position or his job. But today he felt nothing but animosity for Muncie and Abrams; both men equally repugnant weasels who enjoyed pushing employees around because of the power of their positions. But he had a plan to complete, and he simply said, "I missed the bus."

"Watch yourself," Mr. Muncie said.

As Muncie turned and walked away, Walter showed him his middle finger. This surprised Walter since he had always feared the repercussions of making such an obscene gesture. But this time, he felt good about doing it.

The clock on his computer screen read: 8:35. Although the vault had been unlocked since 8:00 a.m., he planned to wait until noon to make his move. That blubber belly, Agnes Farwell, would be eating lunch at her desk near the vault entrance, much too busy stuffing her face to keep an eye on the loose bills that sat in the open compartments. He would courageously walk in, fill his pockets with the bills and leave at his usual time, ostensibly for his lunch. He knew there would be at least fifty thousand just waiting there to be picked up. With his pockets filled, he would go home and attend to Mildred. Then it was hello West Coast sunshine and the start of a new life, devoid of anxiety, trepidation, and doubt.

At ten minutes to twelve, he headed for the vault. Fatso Farwell was stuffing her face just as he had expected, paying him little mind. Inside the vault, he walked slowly, deliberately, to the money compartments. He had no fear of being seen as he scooped up all the bills and stuffed them into his jacket pockets, then turned and walked casually out of the vault.

Andy Holloway wasn't standing in his usual corner as Walter approached the front entrance. He was in front of the doors with his gun drawn, pointed at Walter. "Hold it there, Culpepper!" Holloway said.

Holloway was an incompetent fool, trying to be a hero, a meager impediment to his plans. Neither he nor his gun could stop Walter now.

Walter saw his chance. He dodged to his right, easily bypassing the older, slow-moving Holloway, and darted through the bank doors and out to the crowded street. He pushed his way through the myriad of noontime people and looked back to see Andy Holloway down on one knee, his gun aimed, ready to fire.

A shot rang out, sending people screaming and scurrying for cover. At the sound of a second shot, a bullet zipped by Walter's left ear, missing him by inches. But what had he to fear? He couldn't be killed by a bullet. He couldn't die by any means, other than old age. He began to laugh, realizing his power, his courage, his invulnerability, and that stupid Andy Holloway, firing into a crowd of people on a busy noontime street.

He made a quick left and disappeared down a narrow alley.

***

Mr. Reaper

He arrived home after midnight. From behind a stand of trees, he scanned his house and grounds for any uniformed police or detectives skulking around, waiting for him to show up. He saw none. Perhaps they had been there and gone, while he was at the airport purchasing a one-way ticket to the west coast for the following morning. Satisfied all was clear, he entered the house through the back door and walked quietly up the stairs. He and Mildred had been sleeping in separate bedrooms for the past six months. Mildred had insisted, and he was more than happy to take his leave and deliver himself from the agonies of her incessant snoring.

He went to his room and packed a bag. He put two hundred dollars of the stolen money in his wallet, wrapped the rest in his underwear and locked it in his suitcase. It was well past two a.m. when he put on his work boots, a long sleeve flannel shirt, a pair of jeans, and a rain jacket. A light rain had begun to fall, and the wind outside his window was beginning to pick up. Nonetheless, he would not be deterred by an impending storm. Tonight he would rid himself of Mildred.

He grabbed the pillow from his bed and stepped into the hallway. He walked softly through the darkness toward Mildred's room at the end of the hall. As he approached her open door, he could hear her labored snoring and see the outline of her figure lying on the bed. As he walked into the room, the sound of thunder rumbled overhead.

Mildred stirred.

He waited.

Mildred stirred again.

He waited again.

It was nearly a full minute before he was able to move closer to the bed. Standing above her, he held the pillow out in front of him. A matter of inches made the difference in solving all his problems.

Do it now, he told himself, *and your troubles are over. Do it now! Do it now!*

Mr. Reaper

He pushed the pillow down quickly against Mildred's face. She squirmed and let out a muffled cry. Pressing his entire weight against the pillow, he waited as she thrashed about, kicking and writhing under the blanket in a desperate attempt at freedom. He held the pillow firm until her agonizing cries became muffled whimpers and then stopped. Her body lay quiet and still. He waited before lifting the pillow to be certain the deed was done.

He looked down into his wife's open, vacant eyes. Her mouth distorted in a portrait of desperation as she gasped for her final breath. He leaned over and put his ear to her chest...no heartbeat, no breathing. He checked her pulse...none. Mildred was dead, and he was glad of it. Casually, he tossed the pillow onto the floor. There was no reason to hurry. Slowly, methodically, he wrapped Mildred's body in the blanket. He removed a length of rope from his pocket and made several loops around the blanket at her ankles. Then he made several wraps around her waist, securing her arms against her body. He tied the remaining length around her neck to hold down the corner of the blanket which he had strategically placed over her head and face.

Satisfied, he lifted the body over his shoulder and carried it downstairs into the kitchen. He removed a flashlight from a hook by the back door, then stepped out into the darkness and headed for the woods.

The rain was heavier now and steadier. The ground was quickly turning to mud, making it more difficult for him to carry Mildred. He wiped the rain from his glasses as he trudged deeper into the woods, the mud sucking at his boots as he pushed through the twisted mess of trees and undergrowth, undeterred by the wind and rain and unafraid of the darkness.

It amused him that he was doing this. In the past, he would never have ventured into the woods at night. But now he was king of the forest, the Robin Hood of Sherwood, afraid of nothing that he might encounter. It emboldened him to complete his plan and get on with his life, to face the world unchallenged.

Lightning illuminated the landscape like a July fourth celebration, allowing him to see the small hill and the cave through the blowing tree limbs, not far ahead.

He paused to catch his breath before continuing and shifted Mildred to his other shoulder. As he did, he stumbled on a patchwork of ground cover. Mildred slid from his shoulder and fell to the muddy ground. He looked down at her angrily and shouted that she was a "*burdensome bitch*". Trouble to him, even in death. But he wouldn't let her interfere with his progress. He had to get her into the cave. The success of his plan was contingent upon killing his wife and concealing her body forever.

He slid his fingers under the ropes that bound her and pulled hard trying to get the corpse back onto his shoulder but the weight of her body and the rain-soaked blanket he had wrapped her in had become too much of a burden for him to lift. When he tried wrapping his arms around the bundle, his feet slipped causing him to fall face forward into a pool of brown water. He tried to catch his glasses as they slid from his face, which only caused him to drop his flashlight. He retrieved his flashlight quickly but was unable to find his glasses in the dark swirling water. He had to find them. He couldn't continue without them. He ran his fingers through the cold water, pushing aside twigs and leaves and small stones, digging his fingers in the mud until, at last, he felt the metal frames beneath the water. He hoped the lenses hadn't shattered. Struggling to his feet, he examined the lenses as he wiped them clean. They were unbroken. He placed them carefully over his eyes as he thought about what to do next.

Looking down at Mildred lying at his feet, he felt his hatred for her swell within him. She was making this more difficult for him. Just as she had always made things difficult for him. But things were different now. Unchallenged by her unreasonable demands, he could do what was right for him. He would give her no considerations. She had never considered his feelings. It wasn't enough that he had taken her life. He needed to

Mr. Reaper

humiliate her even in death. Pay her back for the ridicule and embarrassment she had brought him all those years.

He smiled as the idea came to him: *Drag her lifeless body the rest of the way through the filth and mud until he reached the cave entrance.*

The final, lasting retribution was his.

Taking hold of Mildred's ankles, he hauled her dead weight along the ground, advancing no more than a few inches at a time, mercilessly bouncing her head over jagged rocks and gnarled tree roots. He tugged and pulled with what strength he had left. His breathing labored, his vision obscured, and his own body heavy with rainwater. Once he reached the cave, he tried to get Mildred through the entrance. He shoved, he pushed, he grunted, but the blanket he had wrapped her in had become swollen with rainwater and mud, making it nearly impossible for him to get her through the small opening.

One last attempt by Mildred to make things tough for him.

But she wouldn't have her way, not this time. Wrapping his arms around her knees he shimmied her through the opening, head first, progressing slowly, inch by inch, using his entire body weight against her, until with one grand push, she fell onto the cave floor on the other side of the entrance.

He stepped through the opening easily and sat on a large rock, waiting for his breathing to return to normal, his wife's blanketed corpse, still and silent at his feet. He wiped his glasses again, then played his flashlight beam over the deeper, darker recess of the cave. Solid rock and packed soil made up the walls. The ceiling was embroidered with moss and hanging weeds through which rainwater seeped like leaking pipes. The cave was a hellhole of abandonment and isolation. The perfect sepulcher for Mildred to spend eternity.

He dragged Mildred further into the cave and propped her up against a wet wall. He looked down at his dead wife, feeling no remorse for having killed her. Perhaps it was a byproduct of having no fear, or he had inherited a sense of courage he had

Mr. Reaper

never known. Maybe courage and fearlessness are the same thing. He didn't care what they called it. He had made a deal with Mr. Reaper and gotten what he'd wanted. He would leave all his problems right here in this cave. It was time for him to move on. All he had to do now was return to the house, retrieve his suitcase with the money in it and grab a cab to the airport.

He walked back to the cave entrance and watched the rain assaulting the earth in torrents. Lightning flashed in the distance and thunder shook the cave walls around him. He watched the rain washing the earth, just as he was washing away his former life; leaving everything behind: his house, his job, his wife, and this cave, all a part of a bygone existence of despair, monotony and disappointment. He had plans for a long and happy life and nothing could stand in his way now.

He wasn't startled by the sudden clash of thunder and loud rumbling above his head. But instead, he looked up instinctively, as earth and rock dislodged from the ceiling and fell to the muddy floor in front of him. He covered his ears against the deafening sound as he stepped back, helplessly watching the cave entrance disappear before him. In less than a minute, the cave went dark and silent. He raised his flashlight and shone the beam over the pile of wet rocks where the cave entrance had once been.

He thought for a moment, unmoved. *An unexpected turn of events*, he thought. *A negligible setback.* With a degree of effort and smart thinking, he would remove some fallen rocks, creating an opening large enough for him to escape through.

He set his light on the ground and tried to dislodge one of the smaller rocks, confident the others would tumble loose and offer an opening. He clawed between the rocks with his fingers, pried and tugged, but the muddy soil held the stones together like mortar. He continued until the tips of his fingers bled. He tried kicking at the obstruction and pushing with his shoulder against a mosaic of small stones, but they wouldn't budge. Frustrated and out of breath, he relented. He picked up his light and moved the beam around the cave. There was no other exit. The cave-in had blocked the only way out.

He didn't panic. He couldn't panic. Fear was a prerequisite to panic, and he had no fear. Mr. Reaper had seen to that.

"Mr. Reaper," he said aloud as the thought came to him. He would help. He had come when he needed him before.

"Mr. Reaper," he called out. "I need your help." There was a short reverberation within the cave as his words bounced back at him, hollow and empty. He waited; expecting Mr. Reaper to appear out of the darkness, but the cave remained silent, but for the rainwater dripping through the ceiling, He slid down the wet wall and sat on the damp floor, tired and defeated. His flashlight beam fell on Mildred seated against the far wall. He was sure he heard her muffled laughter from inside the blanket. She was mocking him, humiliating him as she had done in the past. "You're a fool," he heard her say. "You never do anything right."

"It's not my fault!" he shouted.

A loud, shrill cackling resounded from beneath the blanket as Mildred began laughing derisively. He walked across the cave floor and hatefully kicked the blanketed corpse several times. "Shut Up!" he said. "You're dead. I don't have to hear from you anymore." But the laughter grew with such intensity that it echoed in the hollow cave. "Shut up! Shut up!" he repeated. He pressed his hands against his ears trying to block out the mockery, the merciless, unyielding denigration he had endured for so long from the dead thing under the blanket that had once been his living wife. Even now, he couldn't escape her vilification.

He held his hands against his ears until the laughter finally stopped, returning the cave to its insidious silence. He took his seat against the opposite wall again. Maybe someone would discover the cave entrance and set him free, he thought. But he knew there was no longer was an entrance, just a mass of rocks and soil that had now become part of the landscape. His whole life had been wishful thinking.

Mr. Reaper

He leaned back against the wall and turned off his flashlight. The engulfing silence was broken only by incessant rainwater dripping from the ceiling onto the cave floor with a rhythmic *splat...splat...splat,* like a clock ticking away the minutes, the hours, the days. How long would it be before his flashlight batteries failed, imprisoning him in total darkness? He felt only anger, frustration, and failure, emotions he had become accustomed to his entire life. He had no fear of being crushed to death. He wasn't concerned that he would eventually use up all the oxygen in the cave or starve to death. He couldn't die by any of those means. Mr. Reaper had seen to that. He turned on his flashlight again and scanned the cave walls and ceiling, in one last attempt to find a hidden crevice or small aperture, anything that might afford him an escape. There was none.

Resignedly, he turned off the flashlight and sat in the darkness. His fate had been sealed. There was no escape, no hope, no future. There was nothing for him now but to remain helplessly trapped, trapped inside this cave with Mildred for a very long time—until he died of old age.

In the darkness, Mildred began laughing again.

Night Work

It's always the dumb ones that get into trouble, the ones foolish enough to go out alone at night and walk down a dark deserted street. This one came out of a brownstone on Forty-second and I watched her walk through a dark alley to get to the next block. She was attractive enough—a tall blonde with a nice figure and a wiggle when she walked that would make any man look twice. These girls all fall into the same category—pretty but dumb—not enough sense to keep out of harm's way in a city like this. Maybe they think rape and murder only happens to strangers they read about in the morning papers, or that it won't happen to them. I suppose it's a little of both. I don't try to figure it anymore. Although, there are times when I ask myself why I do this. I know I'm driven to it for my own reasons, and there are drawbacks—like it being all night work—but, when the thing is done there's a great rush of satisfaction for me.

The night breeze was cold, and I turned up my jacket collar as I followed her, keeping a distance and staying in the shadows. It's not difficult to remain unnoticed. These girls make it easy for predators (I dislike that word; it conjures up images of bloodthirsty animals in a jungle). They make themselves victims, being in the wrong places at the wrong times. That's why I'm successful at what I do. Sure, there's always a risk, but I'm willing to take it. Like I said—they make it easy.

I looked at my watch. It was half-past ten, and I wondered where she could be going at this time of night. People have weird habits and keep strange schedules, but I've learned to follow the patterns of how people live.

She turned onto Montague Street, which was quiet for a Saturday night. The sound of her boot heels echoing off the sidewalk increased as she quickened her steps (as if walking faster made her any safer). I felt that sense of morbid competition rush through me as I picked up my own pace.

At the corner of Forty-third and Montague, she hurried into one of those "open all night" coffee shops. I stood under an awning across the street and watched her hurry to a wall phone and punch up some numbers. The shop was well lit, and it was easy to watch her every move through the plate-glass window. At the counter, an indolent counter clerk flipped the pages of a magazine, while a guy in baggy pants and a hooded sweatshirt sipped a mug of coffee. I thrust my hands into the front pockets of my jeans to keep warm and waited....

As I watched this vulnerable young girl, I thought of Andy and that night almost a year ago, when, as a rookie cop, he lost his life trying to save an innocent girl from an attacker. Losing an only son that way hits a man hard and even the sessions with Doctor Bentley didn't help. He'd said, in time, the anger would subside, but with such a loss, time and even life seem to lose their meaning.

The girl spoke into the phone for nearly a full minute and I noticed baggy pants looking in her direction as if he were more interested in her than he should be. She didn't notice him and after hanging up, scurried passed him and out the front door. My curiosity piqued when I saw him slide off his counter stool and follow her out. He let her trek up Montague for half a block, then flipped his hood over his head and began to follow. She continued up Montague with baggy pants not far behind. It was obvious he had his plans, but I couldn't let him interfere with mine—I owed it to Andy. I stepped off the curb and crossed the street.

Instinctively, I felt for the knife in my back pocket, one of my tools of the trade. You find out which ones work for you and learn to use them efficiently. A gun isn't always the best choice, that's why I use the switchblade, it's easy to conceal and at the push of a button, the six-inch blade is out and it's as sharp as a razor...although, it does leave more of a mess.

At the end of the block, the girl crossed the street and headed into the park, (another big mistake, but typical). Baggy pants jogged into the park and disappeared behind some shrubbery. I watched him scurry from tree to tree, keeping his distance while trying not to lose sight of her. He wasn't very good at concealing himself and if she looked back, she would have easily spotted him. I darted across the street and vaulted a black wrought-iron fence, which paralleled the path where she was walking. There were no lights on this side of the path and it was easy to keep close to the fence and walk in the darkness, while baggy pants jumped from tree to tree like a comic rabbit. The rear entrance to the park opened onto the main street. Traffic was steadier here, and I watched the girl maneuver through it to get to the other side. I stopped behind an iron gate and watched baggy pants dash across the street and conceal himself in a darkened doorway. She reached the sidewalk, turned right and headed in his direction. *He'd be a fool to try something here,* I thought. But then, these amateurs *are* fools, that's why they get caught. I moved out behind a parked car and waited.

The girl walked briskly toward the doorway where baggy pants had dug deep into the shadows. The traffic signal at the corner started a cycle, and each changing color illuminated him. As she got closer to him she walked into a blanket of amber light and I saw him reach into the front pocket of his sweatshirt and bring out a metallic object that reflected brightly for an instant in the headlights of a passing car. I walked to the front of the parked car as he inched out of the doorway and waited for her to pass. I could see he wasn't sure of himself. (The uncertainty of amateurs makes them even more dangerous). As I stepped off the curb, the traffic signal cycled again, and I

Night Work

watched him slither out of the darkness and move in on her. He was just a few feet behind her when suddenly he hesitated. I wasn't surprised when he turned quickly and bolted through a flood of red light down the sidewalk away from her. I watched him zigzag through traffic and disappear into a parade of blinding headlights. Baggy pants had lost his nerve! I'd seen it more than once. "Mr. Horny" gets a crazy idea, then finds he doesn't have the nerve to carry it through—back to the "girlie" magazines.

When I looked back, the girl was entering the front door of an apartment building. I leaned against a tree—it was going to be a long night. Maybe I'd walk back to Forty-second Street and wait. I had had better luck in that neighborhood. As I turned to walk back through the park, the door opened again and the girl stepped out and continued up the street, walking more vigorously than she had before. Maybe tonight wouldn't be a waste. I zipped up my jacket and turned up my collar. The night was turning colder, but the hunt was warming.

***

The bus shelter in front of the Reinhold building was one of those glass-enclosed structures with an aluminum bench inside. It had no lights and only a single street lamp a short distance away illuminated the area. I leaned against a telephone booth at the corner and watched the girl hurry to the shelter where she began pacing. I looked at my watch. She was waiting for the eleven-forty, which I knew took passengers out of the city. I watched her pace for another five minutes until she finally sat on the bench. For the first time, she seemed genuinely afraid by the way she kept looking around and checking her watch every thirty seconds.

I moved along the side of the Reinhold building to set myself up to make my move when the time was right. Traffic was almost nonexistent here, and the street was still

Night Work

and deserted. I watched her pull a cigarette from a pack she removed from her purse and when she lit it the yellow flame illuminated her face and for the first time I could see how attractive she was. Not that I need to know how these girls look. What's important is that she's where she should be—or shouldn't be. Here was this young girl alone in the heart of the city at the time of night when the "creepy-crawlers" come out. That's the reason predators always find a quarry. Like I said—they make it easy.

I was close enough now to move in on her anytime. I stood in the shadows of an alley that separated the Reinhold building from its neighbor and watched as she waited impatiently for the bus. The headlights of a passing police cruiser lit up the shelter, and I pressed myself deeper into the shadows as the cop looked directly at the girl on the bench. I waited until the cruiser continued up the street and turned at a distant intersection before I slipped into the front doorway of the building, which put me about twenty feet directly behind her. From where I stood, I could see the street and sidewalks on both sides of it. There was no traffic or movement other than the girl fidgeting on the bench. Most of the area was in shadow and the street lamps offered little illumination.

As I scanned the facade of the buildings across the street, I spotted what looked like someone running to this side of the street at the corner. I followed the obscure figure until it blended into the shadows of the storefronts. It was obvious the girl didn't notice as she rose from the bench and walked to the curb as if anticipating the arrival of her bus. I checked my watch... she had twenty minutes more to wait.

I thought I saw movement behind a low shrub not far from the bus shelter—or was the night breeze playing tricks? I strained my eyes forward, watched and waited. Suddenly, a dark figure sprang from the shrubbery! Baggy pants was back and barreling toward the bus shelter straight for the girl! He came up behind her, wrapping his arm around her throat. She let out a quick scream that was cut short as he tightened his grip and began dragging her back toward the shadows. I rushed from the doorway, came up behind him and pulled his arm from the girl. He was surprised but turned quickly to me, wrapping his hands around my neck while the girl ran screaming into a corner of the shelter. He was slight but stronger than I'd expected and I had a hard time bringing him to the ground. His bony fingers dug deep into my throat but I was able to pry his sweaty hands away and a quick rap to the jaw dropped him to the pavement. Behind me, I saw flashing lights and knew the uniforms were on the scene. But baggy pants wasn't finished. He kicked up at my legs, knocking me to the ground and was on me in an instant, throwing punches to my face. I brought my arms up to block the blows as two uniforms grabbed him and lifted him off me. I got to my feet, short of breath, as they held him against the building and cuffed him.

Inside the shelter, the girl was near hysteria. When I reached for her, she let out a short scream. "It's okay," I said. She was confused and frightened but allowed me to put a comforting arm over her shoulder.

"Everything's all right," I said. "You're safe now."

She looked up at me and I saw her face soften as I flipped open my ID and showed her my badge.

"I-I can't believe it," she said. "I might have been killed."

"Or worse," I said. "You're a lucky girl."

"But how did you—"

"I've been following you since you left your apartment."

"But I never—"

"I know you didn't."

Behind us, the uniforms had cuffed baggy pants and was loading him into the police cruiser. I gave them a "thumbs up" and they sped off with baggy pants, shouting and kicking in the back seat.

"I'm so ashamed," she said, watching them disappear around a corner. "How stupid I've been."

"We learn from our mistakes," I said, trying not to sound too philosophical.

"I need to get home," she said.

"Don't you have to be someplace?"

"After this?"

"I don't have wheels," I said, "but I'll walk back with you."

We started down the main street toward Montague in the direction of Forty-second. I could see she felt safe walking with me and was glad I had made the offer. After a few minutes of awkward silence, she asked, "Have there been many attacks in this area?"

"Three in almost a year," I said. "All young girls...their throats were cut."

"I had no idea," she said, visibly disturbed by the image. "I didn't read it in the papers."

"We decided to keep it from the press for a while. Most of these 'loonies' like the publicity; it feeds their sickness. The department set up this special squad of plainclothes officers who walk the area with the patrols nearby but out of sight. If a young woman puts herself in harm's way, most of the time, we're quick enough to prevent someone from getting hurt."

"Or killed," she said.

"Our friend tonight was the second arrest we've made; both were young men with special problems."

A misty rain began to fall, and we stopped under an awning.

"There's an alley at the end of the block," she said. "I often use it as a shortcut. I guess it'll be okay now."

I nodded, and we started to walk again. When we reached the end of the block, we turned into the shadows of a narrow passage between two buildings.

"I won't be using this shortcut again," she said, "not after tonight."

"That would be wise," I said.

We were in total darkness now except for the light from the street lamp spilling into the alley at the other end. I walked behind her, being careful not to let her get too far ahead.

Night Work

"I guess I should consider myself lucky," she said, her voice echoing in the darkness in front of me. "How were you able to follow me tonight and be there at just the right moment?"

The amber glow from the street lamp fell on her horrified face as I pinned her against the building and pressed my knife blade against the soft flesh of her throat. "You made it easy," I said.

Silent, Secret

Eddie Schofield was a fool. He had always been a fool for as long as I had known him and it was his foolishness that caused his end.

The summer I turned sixteen, I lived with my parents in the High Street apartments, a twelve-story building with twenty or so three and four-room cubicles, aptly designated, "low income" apartments. Eddie, Ralphie, Carlos and me grew up on High street and although we were tough kids in a rough neighborhood, we weren't criminals; at least we didn't think we were until—as we later found out—Eddie got the idea to rob Old Man Ellis. He'd kept it a secret, so we didn't know about it until the whole thing was over. If he had come to us with it, we would have pounded his head into the pavement until he came to his senses. But Eddie was always a bit different, not mental or anything, just lazy, always looking for the easy way out.

Old Man Ellis lived in our building for as long as I can remember. He mostly kept to himself so no one knew much about him. Ralphie's mom told us he was near eighty and had moved here from Michigan. He rarely left his apartment, except to buy groceries and walk to the corner store in the evening for pipe tobacco; although, sometimes we would see him in the park on Sundays.

That summer, Joey Ellis moved in with his grandfather after Joey's parents split-up and the law couldn't find either of them. He was a good kid, got a job right away at the Food Mart and seemed to get along with his grandfather, all right. He got to know us guys pretty fast, even though we found out right away he liked to throw the bull; I knew he was just trying to impress us with stories about his life on the West Coast and how he was looking for his father and couldn't wait to go back—none of us believed him, anyway.

One hot August night we were pitching pennies against the front stoop when Joey began talking about his grandfather. We had all been shooting the breeze about nothing, when out of nowhere; he began telling us the details—as if we had asked.

When his grandfather was a young man, Joey said, he'd worked as a diamond cutter for a large jewelry firm in New York City. He was earning more than an adequate salary but it seemed an occasional diamond would find its way into his trouser cuff and as the years passed, he had acquired a collection of stones that would make Tiffany's jealous.

I pitched a penny. "And what was he going to do with these diamonds?" I said.

"Sell them and move away with his family where he'd live like a king," Joey said.

"Then, why didn't he?" Ralphie said.

"Because his wife died unexpectedly and his son got married and moved to the West Coast. He was left alone."

"Why would his son leave his father with all those diamonds?" Eddie wanted to know.

"No one knew he had them, except his wife."

It was my turn to pitch again. "I don't believe it," I said. "Why does he live in that small apartment?"

"With all that ice," Eddie said, "he could live anywhere."

Carlos picked up his pennies. "How much are they worth?" he said.

"Half a mil—"

There were a few moments of silence as the words sunk in.

"I don't believe it, either," Ralphie said.

"It's true!" Joey shouted. "I seen 'em!"

Eddie scooped up his pennies and sat on the stoop. He removed a comb from the back pocket of his jeans and ran it slowly through his long black hair, using the reflection from the basement window as a mirror. "Where does he keep 'em?" he said—seriously.

I could see Eddie believed Joey.

"In a tin box, under his bed."

I laughed aloud. "Do you expect us to believe that? An old man with a half o' million in diamonds and he keeps 'em under his bed!"

Carlos and Ralphie laughed too…Eddie didn't.

"Nobody's that dumb," Ralphie said. "Why doesn't he spend 'em?"

"Got nobody to spend them on," Joey said, "And he's got everything he needs. He's an old man."

"I'd show him how to spend 'em," Eddie said.

We put our pennies back into our pockets; it was getting too dark to pitch, and we called it a night. Before I started up the stairs, I looked back through the front door window and saw Eddie on the stoop still talking to Joey. Nothing seemed unusual, except Eddie was talking to Joey without the rest of us there. I watched for almost a full minute until they walked down the street and disappeared around the corner.

The details of the robbery were chronicled in the Sunday morning paper. I sat on the stoop and read the story to Ralphie and Carlos. They listened intently, finding it hard to believe what Eddie had done—and right in our neighborhood.

***

Eddie hid in the darkened hallway and watched Old Man Ellis close the apartment door and shuffle toward the elevator. He waited for him to disappear behind the elevator doors, then with a glance around, headed for the apartment. Slamming his shoulder against the apartment door, he turned the knob hard several times until, with a crack, the door jolted open.

The kitchen counter was cluttered with dirty dishes. The round table in the center of the room was empty except for a small wicker basket filled with fruit. A window on the far wall opened onto a courtyard below and Eddie could see a web of clotheslines stretching from one building to the next. He hurried into the bedroom, knowing the old man would be back soon.

Under the bed, Joey said, in a tin box.

He kneeled beside the bed and lifted the overhanging covers. With his free arm, he reached under and sliced at the air but stirred up only dust. He slid under on his belly and swam around blindly, searching every corner. Scrambling to his feet, he hurried to the other side and searched again.

It had to be there. Joey said it was!

He paused to give the room a quick scan.

The old man must be hiding it somewhere else, he thought; Joey must have been wrong.

Hurrying to the dresser, he pulled out drawers, aimlessly tossing socks and underwear in every direction. In the closet, he pushed the clothes aside and spilled the contents of shoeboxes out onto the floor. The bathroom and kitchen were the only rooms left. He raced along, opening each kitchen cabinet, looking behind cereal boxes and cans of soup. He looked inside the breadbox and in the refrigerator and under the sink and behind the stove. He searched in the clothes hamper and even checked behind the toilet. Frustrated and out of breath, he stood in the silence not sure where to look next.

The whirr of the elevator motor echoed in the hallway. Pressing his ear to the apartment door, he could hear the old man shuffling back down the hall. He couldn't get out now, not without being seen.

He bolted toward the kitchen window and opened it. He would climb out onto the ledge below the window, wait for the old man to leave the room, then climb back in and escape out the apartment door.

Straddling the windowsill, he stepped precariously onto the twelve-inch ledge, pushing the window down just as Old Man Ellis entered the kitchen carrying a bag of groceries. Eddie inched over to one side, keeping out of sight but peering in enough to watch the old man's every move. When the time was right, he'd climb back in and scram out of there.

As he adjusted his footing and tightened his grip on the window frame, he threw a glance over his shoulder at the courtyard six floors below. The cracked blacktop was deserted but for a few pigeons pecking for their dinner. Behind him on an empty clothesline, an array of birds sat like an attentive audience. Their presence made him uneasy as they watched his helplessness with mock indifference. He pressed himself against the building and tilted his head just enough to watch the old man pulling items from the grocery bag and placing each strategically on the kitchen table as if it were important to have all the cans of Campbell's Soup standing together. He watched the tedious process as each item was brought out and carefully placed in its respective order until the table resembled a Chessboard.

The sound of a window opening below brought his attention to someone tossing a handful of bread pieces out onto the blacktop. His feathered audience spiraled down from their clothesline perch and descended on the morsels like hungry vultures. He hugged the building as the wind from their wings beat against the back of his neck.

"Come on, old man," he whispered aloud, "this is torture." The awkward position of his legs caused his body to stiffen, his knees weakened and his fingers ached. Pressing his face against the window frame, he waited…

Moments passed in agony before he saw Mr. Ellis move out of the kitchen and shuffle toward the bathroom. Now he'd make his move. Stretching his neck to be sure the room was empty; he carefully slid his feet along the ledge to center himself in front of the window. Once there, he would slide the window up, climb in and exit the apartment before the old man returned.

Moving his other hand onto the window frame, he began to steady himself when a flutter of wings erupted behind him again. Engulfed in the whirlpool, the force of wind and wings slapped his body as he pressed against the building, squeezing his eyes shut and tightening his grip. His senses swayed like a buoy in a sea of darkness and suddenly, he could no longer feel the ledge beneath his feet. As his body began to free-fall, he grabbed the windowsill and hung there for several seconds, peddling against the brick siding with the well-worn soles of his "sneakers." Frantically, he searched for a footing, trying to relieve his body weight from his trembling fingers. Using every muscle, he pulled himself up enough to peer over the windowsill just as Old Man Ellis was returning to the kitchen.

Shout for help, he thought, the old man would open the window and let him in; he would worry about explanations later.

"Mister, Ellis," he shouted, with what breath he had, "help me!"

The old man picked up two glass jars and pushed them into the back of a cabinet near the sink.

"Mister, Ellis!" he shouted again, "I'm at the window!"

Closing the cabinet doors, the old man retrieved a roll of paper towels and placed them in the cabinet above the stove. Back at the table, he gathered up several large cans and put them on the counter behind him.

Eddie's fingers began to quiver and his shoulder blades burned from stretching under his body weight. He shouted again. "Please, Mister Ellis, open the window, I can't hang on much longer!" A plane flew low over the building drowning out his words. He waited for it to pass before trying again. "For God's sake, I'm sorry," he shouted, even louder than before, "You can't let me fall!"

He pedaled his legs on the building again and pulled up on the windowsill, shouting as loudly as he could, "Mr. Ellis! Out here!" But his words were lost in the wind that whistled passed his ears and the fluttering of bird wings behind him. He hung there helplessly still, awaiting the rescue that would never come.

***

Silent, Secret

They found Eddie's body the following morning in the courtyard. The police investigation took just three days. Detective Moreno from our precinct came and talked with us since we were Eddie's friends. He asked us questions and told us some things that weren't in the newspaper.

When Joey's grandfather walked into the bedroom and saw his things thrown every which way, he knew someone had been in the apartment. Joey called the police as soon as he got home from work. The police knew Eddie was the one who broke in since he'd left his fingerprints all over the place. They figured he'd climbed out onto the ledge when Mr. Ellis came home and was out there for a long while waiting for an opportunity to climb back in; he probably lost his footing and fell to the courtyard below.

We had told Detective Moreno about Joey's story. He said the police searched everywhere but didn't find a box of diamonds. It was possible, he said, Joey took the box and hid it long before he told us the story, hoping one of us would be foolish enough to break into the apartment, taking suspicion off him. That made sense to me since Eddie had been pumping Joey all day for details and Joey seemed more than happy to tell Eddie everything he wanted to know. But, this was all theory Detective Moreno said; there was no way anyone could prove it. No one knew for sure if there was a box of diamonds since one had never been found and Old Man Ellis couldn't admit he ever had one. But Joey Ellis was gone, and we didn't know why. That was for sure. Maybe Detective Moreno's theory was right.

We never saw Joey again after that summer. His grandfather went about as though nothing had happened. He continued his evening walks to the corner store, but we never saw him again in the park on Sundays.

We all felt pretty sad for Eddie. Ralphie asked Detective Moreno why Eddie didn't call for help if he was stuck out on that ledge for so long.

"I suppose he did," Detective Moreno said, "but it wouldn't have mattered. Mr. Ellis is stone deaf."

Guess Joey forgot to tell Eddie that.

Cassie

"You can't let him get away with it," she said.

"But what can I do?"

"You'll have to kill him," she said.

Joe Ganz looked down at Cassie, who was sprawled comfortably on the sofa. *She is beautiful, he thought, with her soft green eyes and blond hair, but she has a sinister mind.*

"I can't kill a young kid," he said.

"If you don't, you'll wind up in jail."

Joe knew she was right. During the time they had been together, Cassie had always given him good advice. She had always been there for him. She was there when he got out of prison and helped him to deal with his parole officer. And if it weren't for her, he would never have gotten through those psychiatric sessions with Dr. Winslow. The doctor had suggested finding a friend, a companion, so he wouldn't be alone. Finding Cassie had been the perfect medicine for him. She helped him physically and mentally and now he wouldn't know how to live without her. He'd always discussed things with her before making a move, considering her advice and ideas, and each job had always come off as planned and without a hitch.

But Tuesday night had been different. He had stopped by the convenience store to buy a six-pack, not a customer in the place, just a pimple-faced high school girl clerking the register. It looked too easy to pass up. One of those things you do without thinking much about it before you do it. And then, his gun was out, and the terrified girl was grabbing bills from the register drawer and sliding them across the counter. She had even given him a cigar box filled with bills that were hidden under the counter. He couldn't help smiling as he reached into the box and stuffed the bills into his coat pocket with the others. He remembered thinking this was the easiest score he'd ever made just as the kid jumped out from the food shelves behind him and blinded him with the light. It was one of those digital cameras with a built-in flash and the kid had taken his picture as he stood there, pointing the gun at the clerk. As he waited for the spots to clear from his eye, the kid bolted out the front door and was gone. When he could see again, he scooped up the rest of the bills from the counter and scrammed out of there.

Back at the apartment, he'd explained everything to Cassie, who wasn't very happy that he hadn't discussed things with her first. "That's how you get into trouble," she admonished, "by trying to think for yourself."

"I didn't plan it," he'd said. "It was an easy take. I got almost five hundred."

He dropped the bills on the coffee table and walked to the kitchen area to get a beer from the fridge. Cassie was annoyed with him, and he hated himself for doing that to her. At the refrigerator, he popped open a can of beer for himself and poured Cassie some cold milk from the gallon as a conciliatory gesture. Cassie loved cold milk. He set the milk on the coffee table in front of her.

"Did you see what he looked like?

"Just a teenaged kid with a camera and then everything was spots."

He sat on the sofa beside her and cuddled her against him. "Don't be upset," he said. "It was a good score."

"One that comes with a ton of trouble," she said. "We'll have to wait and see what happens." She pushed away from him and began to drink her milk.

The next morning he found a copy of the photo which had been slipped under the apartment door. On the back had been written: "$10,000 or I tell" A phone number was scrawled beneath it.

"How did he know where to find you?" Cassie said.

"I don't know," Joe said, pacing the floor.

"Well, he's got you where he wants you," she said. "If we don't give him the money, he'll go to the cops."

"Where we going to get that kind of money?"

"We're not," she said. "That's why you have to get rid of him, and the problem."

Joe had done his share of killing in his younger days when he worked for the mob and the few people he'd done away with deserved it—lowlife con men that would cheat their own mothers to make a quick buck. But this was different; a smart-aleck kid was in the wrong place at the wrong time and got the crazy idea that he could make himself a fortune the easy way. The kid certainly didn't deserve to die for being stupid. He was definitely against it and knew he'd have to convince Cassie to change her mind.

Cassie walked to the front window and stared down at the busy sidewalk. "If he doesn't hear from you, he'll turn that picture in and it's goodbye Joe Ganz Your face will be in every post office in the country. You want to live the rest of your life lookin' over your shoulder?"

Joe looked at the phone number on the back of the photo he was holding. "Maybe there's another way," he said.

"What way?"

"I'll talk to him. Make him a deal, cut him in as a partner, give him a chance to make some big cash."

"Why should he work for it when he can squeeze it out of you with his feet up?"

"If I tell him I don't have the money, make him understand."

"Make him feel sorry for you. Don't be stupid."

She flopped back down on the sofa. "This kid knows he's got a good thing going. As I see it, you got three choices: pay the money, go to jail or kill the kid."

***

He was a scrawny kid, about fifteen with long red hair and freckles, and Joe could see he was not afraid to be there in the alley with him.

"Why are you doing this, kid?"

"For the money."

"I told you there is no money."

"You can get it."

"How?"

"Knock off some more of them candy stores like I caught you doing. You seem pretty good at it, even though it was a cinch for me to follow you back to your apartment. You should be more careful. If I could find you, the cops could find you quicker. Hate to see you arrested before I get my money."

Cassie's right, Joe thought. *The kid knows he's got a good thing going and he's being cocky about it.* For an instant, anger surge inside Joe. He wanted to grab the kid by his throat and shake some sense into him. He had pleaded with Cassie to let him see the kid and try to reason with him. When their discussion nearly turned into a heated argument, she reluctantly agreed. So he had called the number and convinced the kid to meet him in the alley behind the movie theater.

"What do you want all that money for, anyway?"

"My ma needs it."

"Don't your father work?"

"I got no father."

This kid's got problems, Joe thought, *but mine are bigger.*

"I told you, kid, I got nowhere near that kind of money, but maybe we can work something out. I can give you a chance to earn at least that much and more. Come in with me. Help me pull off a few small jobs, we'll split fifty-fifty."

The kid laughed. "I ain't no holdup man," he said, "that's your racket. Besides, if I get locked up, who'll take care of mom?"

Hearing the kid talk like that softened Joe up even more. He sure wasn't making it any easier for him. How bad could this kid be if he worries about taking care of his mother?

Cassie

"Look, kid, you're in way over your head," Joe said. "You're pushing me into a corner. Just give me the picture and forget about it." He reached into his pocket and took out a wrinkled bill. "Take this hundred and split," he said.

The kid glared at the hundred. "If you can whip a hundred out of your pocket—just like that—then you got plenty more somewhere else. I might be young, but I ain't stupid."

"But this is some of that money from the job you saw me pull. I told ya I got no big money."

The kid began to back out of the alley, keeping his eye on Joe. "You got till the end of the week to come up with the cash," he said, "or that picture gets mailed to the cops." Without another word, he turned on his heels and disappeared around the corner.

Joe stood alone in the quiet alley. He had given it his best shot and now he had to go back to the apartment and face Cassie. He knew what her answer to the problem would be.

It was dark by the time he got back to the apartment. Cassie was asleep on the sofa but awoke when she heard him shut the door and flick on the light switch. She yawned and enjoyed a long stretch before she sat up.

"How'd it go?" she said.

He sat on the sofa beside her. "Just like you said, he wants his money. He gave me till the end of the week." She dropped down and put her head on his lap. "He's just a kid," he said, "fourteen or fifteen."

"Don't feel bad about it," she said. "He's giving you no choice."

He ran his fingers gently through her soft hair. "I just wanted to make him understand that he was making a mistake, putting me on a spot, boxing me in, to whack this kid is almost a sin—a big waste of life."

She sat up quickly. "He knew what he was doing," she said. "He got himself into this and he's got to pay the consequences. Would it make any difference if he were forty years old? Fourteen or forty, the situation's the same. You know what you gotta do."

He couldn't argue with her logic. She'd been right from the beginning. There was no other way.

Resignedly, he stood and walked to the phone. He would make the call and set up a meeting with the kid, telling him he had his money. They would meet in the alley behind the movie theater and there he would finish this thing.

After he made the call, he walked into the bedroom and took his 9mm from the top dresser drawer. He checked the magazine—more than enough rounds for this job. As he walked back into the living room, Cassie followed him with a silent stare. He dropped the gun into his coat pocket and walked toward the door. Pausing with his hand on the knob, he looked back at Cassie. *She is beautiful,* he thought *but has a sinister mind.* He smiled, knowing he loved her anyway. Turning the knob, he flipped off the light switch, stepped into the hallway and closed the door behind him.

In the silence of the darkened room, Cassie stretched out comfortably on the windowsill, licked her paws and blinked up at the moon.

Easy Take

The sign in front of Colby's Diner read: NO PARKING ANYTIME. Marty Gannon pulled his Harley beneath it and turned off the engine. He sat breathing deeply the dry southwestern air and letting the afternoon sun warm his handsome face. The cigarette dangling from his lips was unlit and before dismounting he struck a match on the side of his studded boot, lit the cigarette and tossed the spent match into the high grass by the front door. Through his dark glasses his eyes followed the hills and curves of the seemingly infinite roadway, until, like a writhing snake, it disappeared over the horizon. A glance back at the parking area revealed an eighteen-wheeler and an older, well-kept Chevy convertible.

He had stopped here yesterday on his way back to L.A. and got the idea to hit the place because of its remoteness—a "greasy spoon" out on the main highway, twenty miles from the city that catered to truck drivers and the occasional motorist who had lost their way. It would be a cinch to hit since the truckers who stopped here rarely lingered and were more concerned with keeping their schedules.

He pushed open the front door and without removing his sunglasses, gave the place a quick scan. A chipped marble counter paralleled by wooden stools ran along one side of the narrow room. Opposite the counter, beneath a wall of grimy sunlit windows, stood a parade of red vinyl booths, mended in various places with patches of gray Duct tape. Two large ceiling fans cast wavering shadows across the yellowed ceiling. Aside from the two truck drivers seated at the far end of the counter and a young girl alone in an end booth, sipping a cold drink, the place was empty.

As he slid his slender frame onto a stool at the counter, an overweight waitress approached carrying a small pad, pulling a pencil from her hair. "Whattaya have?" she asked.

"Whattaya got?" he asked back, unzipping his leather jacket.

The waitress stepped closer to allow him a better look.

"I got anything you want," she said.

Marty sat unmoved.

"A cheeseburger and a beer."

"No alcohol," she snapped.

"A Coke, then."

He watched her scribble on the small pad, obviously indignant over his disinterest.

"That all?"

Marty nodded, and she turned with no further interest. He watched her waddle back to the kitchen where he knew there was a floor safe. He had seen it yesterday when the guy in the three-piece suit drove up in a black Lincoln and rushed into the diner. He'd walked hurriedly into the kitchen carrying a large manila envelope. When Marty leaned forward enough on his counter stool, he was able to see this guy remove a brick of bills from the envelope and hand it to the cook. The cook opened the door to the safe with a key from his key ring, placed the bills inside and closed and locked the safe quickly. Marty leaned forward now and could see that the same cook was at the griddle today. He had heard the guy say, "Keep it till Monday." Well, it was Friday afternoon and when the time was right, he'd use his gun, prod the waitress into the kitchen and force the cook to open the safe. He'd yank out the phone wire and be gone before anyone knew what went down.

The humming of the ceiling fans broke the silence of the July afternoon. Smothering his cigarette out in the small ashtray on the counter, he looked up at the wall clock.

Somehow, within the rectangular-shaped picture of a Coke bottle and a burger, depicted behind bold letters pledging, "Things go better with Coke!" he was able to decipher that it was nearly 2:00 p.m. He slid a comb from his back pocket and ran it slowly through his long black hair as the waitress emerged from the kitchen with his order. His nostrils flared as she shoved the steaming burger under his nose and slid the frosted Coke beside it.

"Five eighty," she said.

Marty reached into his jacket pocket and felt the large roll of bills; it still had the wide elastic band around it, just like the old man had kept it.

Luck had been with him this morning. As he walked through the alley by the bank parking lot, he saw the old man sitting in his car about to stuff the roll of money into a paper bag and bring it into the bank. He had always done his best work impulsively and as the old man began to climb out of his car, Marty rushed him, shoving him back onto the seat. When he reached for the roll of cash, the old man resisted and Marty had to hit him with his gun. The old man slumped back against the headrest. After counting the bills back at his apartment, he was surprised he had scored five hundred. "Easy take," he'd said.

He had enough money now to split to Vegas, but he knew five hundred wouldn't carry him for long, especially in a town like that. The time was right to hit the diner. So, he'd packed up this morning and headed out for the quick money and then it was off to sin city.

Discretely, he peeled off several bills and stuffed the wad back into his jacket pocket. He placed the bills on the counter.

"Anything else?" the waitress asked, leaning closer in one last attempt at piquing his interest.

"Keep the change," he said.

He munched on the burger slowly, letting each bite linger in his mouth for a while. When he had taken the last mouthful, he licked his fingertips and washed it down with the Coke.

Easy Take

The roar of a passing eighteen-wheeler brought his attention to the highway. Spinning on his stool, he rested his elbows on the counter and looked out at the scorching dryness of the desert. The two truck drivers finished their meal and sauntered passed him and out the front door. Their rig rumbled and coughed as it started, and it took a full minute for the dust to settle in the parking area after they'd pulled onto the highway.

Until now, he had paid little attention to the girl in the end booth. She was the only one in the place and the timing for him to make his move would be now—if she wasn't here. She was attractive enough, with black hair that fell in soft folds over her shoulders and glistened like a patch of satin draped over her head. Marty tapped the top of his sunglasses and peered over the rims. Her dark hair contrasted with the milky whiteness of her skin. She wore a sleeveless dress and sandals and sat reading a paperback while sipping her drink, seemingly oblivious to her surroundings.

He readjusted his glasses and turned away. Focusing on the wall clock's second hand, he followed it twice around, fighting off the desire to look back at her. But before the second hand completed its third swing, his eyes were on her again. He watched her close her book, delicately wipe her thin lips with a napkin and push her empty glass away. Then, as she attempted to pick up her handbag from the seat beside her, she caught it on the corner of the table and most of its contents tumbled out onto the tabletop and floor. It was one of those large canvas handbags, the kind that can carry all of a woman's un-necessities and more.

Within the suddenness of the incident, he caught sight of a gold ring as it bounced off the edge of the seat and rolled aimlessly across the floor, stopping just under his stool. He glanced down at it, then back at the girl who was busy scraping her treasures together. She didn't notice the ring. He could easily pocket it. It might be worth a chunk of change in a Vegas pawnshop. He slid off the stool and flipped the ring into his sweaty palm.

She was examining each item before returning it to the handbag as he approached. He slipped his sunglasses into his front pocket and he could see now that her hair was not black but a deep brown and the light from the front window made it shine like it did. She was even more attractive closeup.

"You missed this," he said, holding the ring up between his thumb and forefinger.

She looked up at him through crystal blue eyes. He looked deep into them, and it was hard for him to turn away. He handed her the ring, and she put it quickly into her bag. "Thank you," she said.

"It rolled under my stool by the counter," he said, sliding onto the seat opposite her.

She continued dropping items into her handbag and spoke without looking at him.

"It isn't worth much, but it has value to me."

He sensed she was shy, not comfortable speaking to strangers. "From around here?" he said.

"I-I'm traveling to Phoenix," she said, "but developed car trouble."

He glanced out the window at the Chevy. "That yours?"

"It won't start. I've called the service station, but they said it would be more than an hour before they could come out."

An hour would screw up his plans. He'd be halfway to Vegas by that time with the brick of money under his belt. Although he wanted to get to know her better, he knew he had to get rid of her quick, without causing suspicion.

"Maybe I could take a look," he said.

She pushed her forearm through the handle of the canvas bag and let it hang by her side. "I don't want to put you through any trouble," she said, "you've been kind already."

"No trouble," he said, as he stood and coaxed her to follow him. "Might be something simple." He walked toward the door. She rose from the booth and warily followed.

***

"Turn the key," he said, lifting the hood.
She turned the key, and the engine moaned.
"Not enough power to turn 'er over," he said.
She climbed out of the car and stood beside him.

A Highway Patrol cruiser sped passed and instinctively he leaned deeper into the engine compartment. Removing a penknife from his boot, he tightened down the distributor cap as the girl moved nearer, leaning into the engine compartment close to him.

"I didn't realize cars were so complicated," she said.

He felt her pressing her body against his. That familiar bolt of excitement rushed through him, but he knew the timing wasn't right for him to get mixed up with a girl. He had to stick to his plan, although she wasn't making it easy.

He reached in deeper and checked for loose connections as he felt her press against him even harder now and he had to push back against her to remove his arm from the web of wires. When he stood up, she stood with him and quickly moved to the driver's door.

"I'll wait for the service people," she said. "There doesn't seem to be anything you can do."

Marty scraped around the battery terminals where there was a build-up of corrosion.

"Give it another try," he said.

She climbed back into the car and turned the key...the engine hummed.

"Corroded battery terminals," he said, slamming the hood shut. "You'll be alright for a while, but have the terminals cleaned."

"If you think I'll be okay," she said, walking back to the diner "I'll phone and cancel the service call or I'll be charged, anyway."

He followed her back into the diner, knowing she was a "monkey wrench" in his plans but half glad that she wasn't leaving yet.

"Thanks again," she said, returning to the booth after she'd made the call. "I don't have enough money to pay you," she said, wiggling into the seat opposite him, "but if you leave me an address, I'll send you something." She slid the handbag into the corner of the booth and leaned her body against.

"Forget it," Marty said, "I'm traveling." He laughed at the thought of leaving a calling card.

"At least, let me buy us a cold drink" she suggested, "a large lemonade."

"I'd like that," he said, knowing it was the wrong thing to do.

A motorcycle rumbled into the parking lot, shattering the shimmering silence of the desert outside. Marty slid into the corner of the booth as he watched a highway patrol cop dismount and enter the diner, smacking road dust from his pants legs. He stepped inside and peered over the rims of his sunglasses, deliberately surveying the place. Marty could feel the cop's eyes burn through him as he paused to look directly into the booth where he and the girl were sitting. Instinctively, Marty felt for the gun in his pants pocket.

First the girl and now this cop—he hoped his luck wasn't running out. Warily, he watched the cop walk to the counter and slide onto a stool. The overweight waitress came out from the kitchen with her pad. "Whattaya have?" she said, leaning over the counter again, more than she needed to. The cop removed his sunglasses, clipped them to his front pocket and buried his head in the menu card. It was easy to see this guy wasn't going anywhere for a good while. He might have to give it up for today and try again—maybe tomorrow. He glanced at the wall clock. "I'll pass on that drink," he said.

"But it's the least I can do since—"

"I need to get going," he said, sliding out of the booth and throwing a cautious look in the cop's direction.

The girl stood and took his hand in a gesture of thanks. She felt warm and smooth and it made him want to stay even more. *Was this good luck or no luck?* he thought. With mixed emotions, he headed for the door. He hadn't even gotten her name.

"Good luck with the car," he said.

She smiled after him as he let the door close behind him.

The Harley thundered in the parking area, rattling the plate-glass windows and kicking up the usual cloud of dust as he maneuvered onto the blacktop. She watched him accelerate down the highway until he vanished into the hilly distance.

***

She sat in the quietness of the diner. The ceiling fans hummed overhead as she opened her handbag and looked in at the large roll of bills with the wide elastic band around it. "Easy take," she thought.

The overweight waitress came out from behind the counter.

"Get you anything?"

The girl looked up with a smile.

"A large lemonade," she said.

The Collectors

"They'll kill me," Collin said. "They mean business."

He was pacing back and forth in front of me, wringing his hands.

"How much do you owe?" I said.

He stopped and looked at me, almost ashamed to admit it, "Twenty-thousand," he said and began pacing again.

With a near-genius IQ, Collin could have climbed higher up the corporate ladder, if it hadn't been for his gambling problem. He had always gambled, but he'd never gotten in this deep. When we roomed together at college, we'd both gambled on a steady basis: Friday night poker games, state lottery tickets, sports betting and the ponies. Even then, I could see it was becoming a problem for him. I suppose I should have said something—being a good friend—but I kept it to myself.

After college, I did a short stint in the military. When I was discharged, I hooked up with Collin again and we split the rent in his city apartment. He'd been working at the Atlantic Bank as an auditor and seemed to ease up on his gambling. I'd landed a job with an insurance firm and the midtown apartment was convenient for both of us.

I was the last to learn Collin had gone back to heavy gambling, most of his colleagues at the bank were already aware of it but I wasn't surprised when he approached me.

I looked at my watch. It was 3:10 in the afternoon. I had an appointment in twenty minutes and didn't have the time nor the desire to discuss Collin's problems.

"You don't want to meet the Capelli brothers," he said, very seriously, "they're the collectors."

"The collectors? You mean, they collect for—"

"That's right," he said. "And you only get two chances. The first time they show up, you're reminded very politely how much you owe. If you pay, you never see them again. If they need to come back a second time, and you don't pay, you *really* never see them again—or anyone else."

"They kill you?"

"If you don't pay."

"That makes no sense," I said. "If they kill you, they never get their money."

"It's not about the money," he said. "It's about setting an example for the next guy. It may be illegal but it's their business, their livelihood, they can't let it collapse."

I picked up my raincoat from the back of the chair and slipped into it. "Well, you screwed up good this time," I said. "You shouldn't have gotten in over your head."

"I don't need your criticism," he snapped. "I need your help."

"You need help," I said, "but not from me."

Collin and I hadn't been getting along as well as we use to since he'd started dating Pamela, my ex-girlfriend. Oh, things were definitely over between Pam and me, but it irked me that he'd started dating her even before the paint was dry, so to speak. And the way he'd tried to keep it from me really bugged me. Dr. Wheeler said losing Collin's friendship wouldn't help my mental state any. He's a good man and has been helping me with my problem since my discharge. To lose a good friend would only unravel much of what he had done, he said. It was important for me to keep a good mental balance. He suggested I work at it.

"I've got to do something fast or I'm a dead man," Collin continued. "You don't know what it's like knowing you might be killed. I freeze at every sound in that hallway. I'm always looking over my shoulder. It's like being haunted by a ghost that's everywhere."

"Have they been to see you, yet?"

"No, but they will be soon."

"Well, even if I had the money, I wouldn't give it to you. You need a lesson."

"This is no time for lessons," he said. "My life's on the line."

He walked to the kitchenette and nervously mixed himself a drink.

"You shouldn't drink so much," I said, but didn't know why I'd said it since I didn't care how much he drank. I'd have to ask Dr. Wheeler about that one.

"Maybe you could make a deal," I offered.

"They don't make deals."

"What about the bank?"

"They won't give me a loan for that amount."

"There must be another way," I said.

He looked at me thoughtfully.

"You're good with figures. I'm sure there's a way of shifting numbers around in your favor."

He sat down on the sofa with his drink, musing over the idea. "There *are* ways of moving money," he said.

I checked my watch again. It was 3:20. Now that I'd gotten the ball rolling, I was confident Collin would find a solution.

"I need to see a client," I said, as I walked toward the door. "You'll have to work this out yourself."

"Thanks for nothing," he said.

***

It was 5:00 p.m. when I got back to the apartment. It began to rain earlier and the rain beat heavily against the windowpanes as I entered. A roll of thunder rumbled the ceiling as I closed the door behind me. Collin was at the desk jotting down figures on a legal pad. "Lock it," he said. I turned the deadbolt and walked toward him. As I approached, he removed a #10 envelope from his inside jacket pocket and dropped it on the desk.

"What's that?"

"The answer," he said.

I picked up the envelope and slid back the flap. A bundle of hundred-dollar bills a half-inch thick hit me in the face. My eyes widened at their pristine newness.

"Where'd you get it?"

He took the envelope from me and stuffed it back into his pocket. His face glowed with what he believed was his own cleverness. In the short time, I'd been gone, the boy genius had come up with a solution.

"If you get caught," I said, "you're looking at heavy jail time."

"I've got nine months to put it back before the government auditors show up," he said. "I do the monthly audit so there'll be no problem keeping the numbers straight until then. Besides, I'd rather do jail time than face the collectors."

"How much?" I said.

"Twenty-thousand," he said…"just enough."

I walked around the desk closer to him. "More than enough," I said. I removed the gun from my pocket, pointed it at his chest and fired twice. A clash of thunder exploded above us and rolled away, carrying the sound of gunfire with it. Collin looked at me for a moment with disbelief, then fell to the carpet. I leaned over him and removed the envelope from his pocket. He had come through; I knew he would. Lying there, he looked serene, almost carefree and I couldn't help wondering how Pamela would react when she found out—but then, what did I care?

I dropped the gun back into my pocket. I'd get rid of it after I left the apartment. When I returned I would notify the police, explaining how I'd found Collin when I arrived home from work. The circumstances would be typical—a heavy gambler had owed money, couldn't pay, and got what was coming to him.

I removed the bills from the envelope and began counting them carefully. I had to be sure. After all, I had a debt to pay too, and the collectors had already been to see me once.

Red Rose, Dead Rose

There was blood everywhere in the kitchen; it trickled down the cabinet fronts and spotted the refrigerator door; it was smeared across the windowpane like an abstract painting and there was a dark puddle on the tile floor beneath the cat. Hilda was perched on the windowsill; when she saw Henderson, she flew across the room and landed on his shoulder. Affectionately, she began rubbing her feathered forehead behind his left ear with the contriteness of a schoolgirl caught with her hand in a cookie jar.

"You've been bad," Henderson said, wiping Hilda's beak with his handkerchief.

The cat lay on the floor under the table, its pleading gray eyes staring blankly at the yellowed ceiling. The snow-white fur was matted and soaked with crimson, and the streams bubbling from its nose and ears told Henderson there was nothing he could do. It didn't take him long to realize Hilda had learned to unlatch her cage door.

Although large birds with beaks and talons of extraordinary strength, Macaw parrots are regarded as docile and lovable. Hilda was such a bird with no inordinate traits—other than her hatred for the color red. Henderson realized this eccentricity when the color red became the common denominator of the few outbursts of aggression Hilda had had. The first occurred last winter while he was reading by the fireplace. Hilda, perched quietly on the back of his armchair, suddenly began screeching into his ear, digging her beak into his neck and shoulder while flapping her wings widely. When he dove from his chair, she flew after him, driving her talons into him repeatedly until he was finally able to take hold of her and place her back into her cage. The red shirt he had been wearing was torn and punctured at the shoulder and the back of his neck was wet with blood. The significance of the color meant nothing to him until weeks later. While he was passing Hilda's cage carrying a notebook with a bright red cover, she went into a rage, clinging to the bars, screeching and beating her beak against them repeatedly. After he'd put the notebook in a desk drawer, she became her usual self. There was no doubt about it, for some reason—unknown to Henderson—Hilda had begun reacting insanely to the color red.

Rose adopted Fluffy soon after the marriage. It was a simple house cat and although Henderson had never been a cat lover, he tolerated it for Rose's sake.

Hilda had been a true companion to Henderson long before he met and married Rose, and they had nurtured a mutual affection for each other. By nature, Macaws are fiercely loyal to a single owner. Rose couldn't understand this.

"It's not that she doesn't like you," he'd said.

"That bird hates me!" she'd shouted.

"Hilda can't hate," he'd said. "She lives by instinct like other animals."

"Red Rose! Red Rose!" Hilda added, from her cage in the living room.

Red Rose was an affectionate nickname Henderson had given Rose while they were dating and during their early years of marriage. Although Hilda wasn't a great talker, she had picked up the phrase quickly and had been repeating it capriciously since then. Coming from her, Rose regarded it as mockery and antagonism.

They'd had the same argument many times during their four years of marriage, and it was obvious that Hilda—through no fault of her own—had driven a wedge between Rose and Henderson. Rose began each argument with complaints about Hilda but always included criticisms of their marriage: no children, no friends, and never enough money. He worked long hours at the library and although his salary was meager, it was certainly enough for them to live comfortably. Rose disagreed. No matter how understanding he'd tried to be, nothing satisfied her—short of his giving up Hilda—which wasn't an option. But it was Rose's unwarranted jealousy over his attention to Hilda that took him from annoyance to anger to hatred for her. "You think more of that bird than you do of me," she'd said. She was right. His affection for Rose had waned and her belligerent attitude only drove him closer to Hilda.

And now, what Hilda had done to Fluffy would make things worse. He knew he'd have to make it look like the cat had gotten out of the house and was unable to find its way back. He'd have to clean up the mess and get rid of the dead animal before Rose returned from shopping.

He put Hilda back into her cage in the living room and returned to the kitchen. He picked up the cat by its collar and dropped it into a plastic garbage bag. The red collar had been its misfortune.

After wiping the kitchen with cleaner and paper towels, he dropped the towels into the bag with the cat and tied a knot at the top. The acreage of woods behind the house would be the perfect place to bury the cat. Carrying the bag through the garage, he grabbed a shovel and headed for the woods. He finished the sordid task, returned the shovel and was washing his hands when Rose returned from shopping.

He sat at the kitchen table, adjusted his glasses and opened a newspaper, just as Rose squeezed her abundant hips through the back door carrying two bags of groceries. *She had never been a beauty queen,* he thought, watching her struggle through the doorway, *but she had always had a good figure before she let herself become the "Pillsbury dough girl".*

"Don't just sit there," she snapped.

Henderson got up, took the bags and carried them to the table.

Rose hung her coat on the back of a chair and began emptying the bags.

He noticed she hadn't closed the door behind her but didn't mention it, knowing how much she disliked opened doors, fearing Fluffy might wander out. When she did notice the opened door, she ran to it, kicking it closed in anger. "This place will be the death of me!" she shouted.

I should be so lucky, he thought.

"Red Rose!" Hilda said.

That evening, Rose made a simple dinner. They sat at the table in silence, which had become their usual manner, until Rose finally looked up with concern.

"Have you seen Fluffy?" she said.

"Not since this morning."

She stood quickly and began searching the rooms, calling the cat by name. She opened the front door and called out, then ran to the rear door and called again. She rushed up the stairs and searched the bedrooms, opened the garage door and shouted into the darkness. When she returned to the kitchen, she was out of breath. "Fluffy's not in the house," she said.

"Perhaps, when you left the door open…"

It took several weeks for Rose to resign herself to the fact that Fluffy wasn't coming home. For days she stood on the front porch and called for the cat, until she finally gave up the ritual, conceding Fluffy was gone forever.

Henderson showed little sympathy for Rose during the following weeks and Fluffy's absence caused her to become more envious of his bond with Hilda. Rose's attitude toward them became intolerable, unbearable. There was no living with it—or her. Henderson knew the time had come to rid himself of Rose. Three *was* a crowd and without her Hilda and he would have a better life.

Red Rose, Dead Rose

He spent days thinking of ways to accomplish the deed. There were the conventional means, of course: shooting, stabbing, poisoning or strangulation (if he could get his fingers around that flabby neck) but they all seemed too messy and he might not have the courage to carry them through. Suffocation seemed to appeal to him most. A well-stuffed pillow pressed firmly against the face for a few minutes and it was done, with little physical contact and no mess to clean, just the body to dispose of and the woods behind the house would suffice for that business.

One night, after midnight, carrying his pillow at his side, he walked gingerly across the carpeted hallway to Rose's room. He and Rose had been sleeping in separate bedrooms ever since she put on the weight and developed an annoying wheeze when she breathed, which made it impossible for him to sleep. Pushing the door back to Rose's room, he entered the total darkness. Guided only by her rhythmic wheezing, he walked to the side of her bed and held the pillow just above her head.

He would only need to push the pillow down hard against her face and hold it firmly until she stopped fighting, squirming, kicking, wheezing. With trembling hands, he slowly lowered it to within inches of her face. *Do it now! A moment of courage and your troubles are over.* But his resolve weakened as the image of Rose writhing beneath the pillow with muffled cries of agony flashed before him. Disheartened by his lack of courage, he walked silently out of the bedroom, wondering how he'd find the strength to accomplish what he needed to do. As he moved quietly back down the hallway, he could still hear Rose wheezing in the darkness behind him.

The solution came to him the following morning while cleaning Hilda's cage. He supposed he should give Hilda credit since the idea had come from her. She had always been there for him and he knew he could count on her help in finding a solution. It was a simple, foolproof plan, one that required intelligent planning more than unfaltering courage. He would carry it out this weekend, which would be his and Rose's fourth wedding anniversary. Feeling the weight of a great burden lifted from him, he gave Hilda a thank you kiss on the soft feathers of her forehead and placed her back into her cage.

For the remainder of the week, he showed an unusual amount of thoughtfulness toward Rose. She was, at first, suspicious, but his persistence convinced her he was genuinely concerned for their marriage and wanted to turn things around.

Saturday night came quickly, and all preparations had been made. He had built an inviting fire in the fireplace, and Rose had prepared a satisfactory dinner. Although wary of his new attitude Rose seemed more at ease with herself and although she kept her distance from Hilda, her habitual nagging over the bird subsided. But Henderson wouldn't be fooled. He knew she was reacting to his phony sentiments and clever manipulation. Inwardly, she was the same jealous demon.

After dinner, they teamed to do the dishes, then settled down on the sofa in front of the hearth. He forced himself to cuddle with her as they sat in the shadows watching the yellow and orange flames dance on the cut logs in a pseudo-romantic setting. In the darkness at the other end of the living room, Hilda sat motionless in her cage; her head tucked neatly beneath her wing in quiet slumber, with one eye she watched them like an attentive audience.

"I have something for the occasion," Henderson said when the moment was right.

He walked to the hall closet and brought back a gift box and placed it on her lap.

"What is it?" she said.

"An anniversary gift," he said, trying to sound sincere. "Open it."

He stood back while she unwrapped the box and lifted out the beautiful satin evening robe he had purchased for her that morning. She stood and held it in the air. "How could you afford this?"

"It doesn't matter," he said, "try it on." He helped her slip her flabby arms into the wide sleeves while struggling to drape the robe over her bulky shoulders.

"Such a long belt," she commented.

"It wraps twice around the waist and ties off on the side," he said. "It's the latest fashion."

He reached his arms around her ample waist and wrapped the belt around twice, tying a double knot at her side.

"It's a bit snug in the shoulders," she said, "but I can use a new one."

"It's very pretty," he said, "but it does make you look heavier than you already are."

He was sure he'd get the reaction he wanted.

"Is that all you have to say?" she shouted.

"Well, you could lose a few pounds," he continued.

"I don't know why I let you do this to me. You're as cold and unfeeling as that bird of yours."

"But I'm sure if you just cut back a bit on deserts you would—"

With this, she picked up the empty box and hurled it at him like a Frisbee. When he ducked, it crashed against the living room wall startling Hilda who began jumping inside her cage and fluttering her wings. "Red Rose! Red Rose!" she screeched.

Henderson took his cue and started for the front door. "I've had enough," he said, grabbing his jacket off the rack and flipping the light switch up to flood the room with brightness.

"I tried to make tonight special, but you spoiled it." Pulling the door open, he rushed out onto the front porch, slamming the door hard behind him. Alone in the moonlight, he smiled, amused by his own cleverness. In a short while he would be rid of Rose and her nagging, bickering, and complaining forever.

He let a few moments pass before inching closer to the window and peering in at Rose. She was standing by the sofa tugging at the robe, trying frantically to loosen the double knot he had tied securely around her waist, the flames from the fireplace reflecting brilliantly against the beautiful sheen of red satin she wore.

He slipped into his jacket and stepped off the porch. As he started down the walkway, he could hear Hilda's familiar litany from inside the house. "Red Rose! Red Rose!"

Red Rose, Dead Rose, he thought, laughing to himself. He turned up his collar and zipped his jacket. The night had turned cold, but he would only need to walk a few blocks before returning. He knew it wouldn't take Hilda long to unlatch her cage door.

Beware, The Willow Wood!

Andy snapped the reins for "Old Johnny" to get up a bit as he turned the wagon onto the Oldwick Road. He tried looking ahead; but even in his fear, he couldn't keep his eyes from darting a look into the wood. He could smell the dankness as the wagon passed through a cold shadow where the trees blocked out the afternoon sun and he became acutely aware of the silence—no sounds from birds or insects, just the squeak of the wagon wheels and "Old Johnny's" clip-clop.

Andy turned eleven that summer, that age when a boy can foolishly believe he has become a man. And although he gloried in his self-appointed manhood—secretly, he had never been more terrified of anything than that acreage of trees blemishing the rolling hills of Pennsylvania's farmland.

From his bedroom window, Andy could see the Weeping Willows on the distant hillside, their dangling arms reaching to the ground, swaying in the moonlit breeze. Each night, he pulled down the shade and drew the curtain but he knew the trees would be there in the morning, searching…reaching…waiting for someone to pass beneath them so they might snatch them up.

Mikey couldn't see the trees from his bedroom, but Andy's eight-year-old brother wasn't very much afraid of anything and didn't quite understand what Father Corrigan was saying at the end of each Tuesday night bible class.

Andy could still see the Father standing before the students in his black robe with the gold crucifix stitched below his left shoulder like a badge, shaking an admonishing finger as he spoke: "Beware the willow wood," he would say, "and dare not stray off the Oldwick Road on your way to or from church. For those who have sinned will be snatched up by the tree servants and held tight until Satan himself comes to take them to Hades."

Andy was sure that meant me. There was the time Bobby Brenner lost his pocketknife and Andy found it the next day by the barn. He would have given it back if Bobby's Grandfather hadn't given him another so quickly. Then there was Sarah Hutchins's Sunday hat. The boys had snatched it from her head and tossed it about like a ball. Andy recalled laughing with the others even though tears rolled down Sarah's cheeks.

He wouldn't admit it then, but Andy was sure he was a sinner.

That's why he wasn't eager to make that delivery to the church on Saturday as his father had requested. he knew he'd have to travel the Oldwick Road passed the willow trees, the only way to and from the church.

"Father Corrigan will need six crates of eggs for the congregation breakfast this Sunday morning," his father said. "I'm sure you're responsible enough to make the delivery, Andrew." He ruffled his son's blond hair, looking for a sign of reassurance, but Andy offered none.

Since taking a spill off the tractor and fracturing his leg, Andy's father had been depending on Andy to help with the farm chores. Especially since Uncle Harlan had gone to New Castle to visit his ailing daughter and wasn't sure when he'd be back. Since losing his wife, Uncle Harlan had been living in the attic rooms and helping around the farm. He was like a second father to Mikey and Andy and Andy had never mentioned his fear of the wood to him or anyone else and didn't want it known now while his father was counting on his help.

That afternoon, after Andy had hitched "Old Johnny" to the wagon, his father, leaning painfully on his crutch, instructed him to lay a horse blanket in the bed of the wagon and load the crates of eggs so the blanket would cushion them during the rough ride. With the wagon loaded, Andy climbed into the seat next to Mikey and took the reins. His mother hurried out of the house and kissed them on our cheeks. "Now don't dilly dally," she'd said. "You should be back long before dark." She smiled as she lifted the bottom of her flowered apron and wiped a tear from the corner of her eye. Mama seemed happy and sad at the same time, Andy thought.

"Your mother is right," his father said. "Those eggs need to keep cool else they'll spoil."

"Keep an eye on Mikey," his mother added. "And don't let him carry any eggs."

"We'll be okay," Andy said, trying to sound responsible. He snapped the reins, and the mare pulled the wagon through the front gate into the open road…in the direction of the willow wood!

***

The sun was low in the afternoon sky when Andy turned the wagon onto the Oldwick Road. The wood was dark and he couldn't see through the trees, Andy felt that familiar bolt of fear bristle the hairs on the back of his neck. Instinctively, he felt the front pocket of his overalls for his pocketknife. Mikey sat beside him, unconcerned, munching caramel candy out of a bag Mama had given them for the trip.

Father Corrigan was waiting by the side door of the rectory as they approached, and Andy felt a sense of comfort in seeing him. He looked different in his worn jeans, denim shirt and work boots, but as they got closer, Andy saw it was the same Father Corrigan with his short-cropped yellow hair and big smile.

"Well, you boys made it," he said, "with no broken eggs, I hope." He ran his hand over the crates as if he could tell if there were broken eggs inside.

"Papa says to get'em cool else they'll spoil," Andy said, climbing down and tying off to the wrought-iron fence. Mikey jumped down, spilling caramels into the high grass. He stooped over quickly to retrieve them.

"We'll do just that," the Father said, patting Mikey on his backside. "Hold that door open, 'mister helper' and we'll get them inside." Mikey retrieved his last caramel, opened the door and leaned his small body against it.

Andy and the Father carried the crates down a long corridor into a stainless steel kitchen where the Father placed them inside a huge refrigerator. After closing the door like a vault, he turned to Andy. "Come to my office, Andrew," he said, "I have something that will interest you."

"Mama says we should get right back with no 'dilly-dally'."

"You won't be long," he persisted.

Andy got the feeling this was something he should not be doing as he pulled Mikey by his shirtsleeve and followed the Father to the end of the corridor.

Inside his office, the Father removed a small wooden box from the top drawer of his desk. "Open it," he said.

Andy wondered what Father Corrigan could have that would interest him as he lifted the lid. Inside, he saw an assortment of colored rocks. The Father knew how much Andy liked collecting rocks and how he had discovered a wide variety digging around the farm.

Andy scanned these treasures, wide-eyed with wonder until he saw nestled in a corner, the largest of them, with its brilliance reflecting the light from the office window—it was quartz! That elusive beauty he had yet to find to complete his collection. Andy lifted it into the air, turning it between my fingers, unable to take his eyes from it for a long while. He stood mesmerized by its pristine beauty until he was brought back to reality by the knowledge that the rock didn't belong to him. Where did the father find it? Was there a place to dig, nearby?

With excited anticipation, he turned his head filled with questions but found myself facing an empty room! Where had Mikey, and the Father gone?

He placed the quartz back into the box and walked out into the corridor. He called to Mikey but heard only the echo of his own words bouncing off the tiled walls. Mama would have a fit if she knew he let Mikey out of his sight. But…he was safe with Father Corrigan. He probably had to whiz and the Father took him to the boy's room. At the end of the corridor, Andy leaned my shoulder against the boy's room door, just enough to poke his head inside. "Mikey, you here…?" His answer was the syncopating sound of a dripping faucet. He let the door close and jogged down the corridor, pushing through the rectory door where "Old Johnny" was waiting outside. He called again, "Mikey! Father Corrigan!" Across the road, he could see the willow trees, their arms swaying ominously in the evening breeze. It's like the entrance to Hell, he thought. As he listened, he was sure he could hear them whispering his name, beckoning him to come to them.

Then he saw "Old Johnny's" ears perk up and he listened harder. A sound was coming from the trees and it sure sounded like Mikey calling. Forgetting his fear, he darted across the road. "I hear you, Mikey!" he shouted as he ran, but with each courageous step he took, his apprehension increased. Torn by the unknown evil before him and the knowledge that his brother needed him, he stopped short of the entrance to the trees.

As he stood staring into those portentous shadows, he thought of his father and the trust he had placed in him to make the egg delivery and keep a close watch on Mikey. And of his mother, who was so happy to see her eldest son taking on adult responsibilities that it brought a tear to her eye. He mustered these thoughts into a bundle of courage, took a deep breath and bolted through the dangling arms awaiting him, swinging his arms and trying not to get caught up. As he ran, he could feel the bony fingers of the tree servants scratching at the back of his neck, trying to grab hold and keep him for Satan, but he fought his way up the hillside until he stopped to rest behind a large tree. Only his labored breathing and the hissing wind moving through the treetops broke the silence. He was afraid and trembling and wanted to run again, run as hard and as fast as he could and keep running straight passed the willow trees until he came out on the other side. But Mikey was in here somewhere.

Where was Father Corrigan? He must have heard Mikey. "Andrew! Andrew! There it was again, coming from up the hill. Andy started running again, darting from tree to tree like a frightened rabbit, trying to avoid the arms reaching down for him.

It was darker here than it had been when he entered. The sun had set quickly and the full moon hung like a new silver dollar in the night sky, but he pushed his way deeper into the wood, forgetting Father Corrigan's warning until he stopped, stiff with terror at what he saw ahead of his. Shafts of moonlight had sliced obliquely through the willow limbs and pierced the earth floor like silver spikes. They stood like an embedded army, trying to keep me from getting to Mikey. "Signs of the Devil!" Andy said aloud, expecting the demon to appear at any moment. Was he too late? Did the trees servants snatch Mikey already? But… Mikey wasn't a sinner. He didn't know how to sin. And then, he remembered, *he* was the sinner, and the Devil wanted *him*!

He bolted between the silver spikes and ran to a larger clearing where he dropped beside a fallen tree. Squeezing his eyes shut, he buried his face in his folded arms, hoping, when he looked up, the nightmare would be over. But, the nightmare was just beginning. When he raised his head, he saw on the crest of the hill, engulfed in an aura of shimmering moonlight, a makeshift wooden shack, windowless, with a single door swinging on its hinges. The hissing wind became a crescendo of howling whirlwind as the debris it carried encircled the shack as if protecting it from intruders. "Mikey!" he shouted." You in there?" If Mikey answered, his cries were lost in the turmoil of wind and debris and Andy knew he would have to go into that shack. What he might find inside only added to his terror. Then he remembered, he had with him the bit of courage he needed—his pocketknife. He pulled the knife from his pocket and with trembling fingers, opened the four-inch blade, sucked in a lungful of damp air and moved toward the shack.

As he pushed against the wind, he saw Mikey appear out of the darkness of the doorway. With tear-filled eyes, he called to Andy. Confused and frightened, he moved away from the shack as Andy hurried toward him, slashing at the groping arms that tried to keep him from his brother. Andy ran until his aching knees let him down, causing him to stumble over a tangle of roots and fall face down into the dirt. He got to my feet quickly but froze—wide-eyed with disbelief at what he saw before me. A black-robed specter was emerging from the shack like a huge bat; its fluttering wings aided by the whirlwind as it barreled toward him and pushed him to the ground again. *This is the Devil*, Andy thought, *come to take me!* Father Corrigan's words echoed in his head as he struggled under the weight of the black shroud…"Beware, the willow wood!"

He grimaced when gnarl-knuckled fingers, tipped with black talons, appeared from beneath the shroud and pierced his shoulders. Mikey's cries continued and Andy felt myself weaken as terror brought him to the point of panic. The wind howled around him, the trees waved their arms above me and Mikey's cries grew louder.

And then, he heard Uncle Harlan calling his name and he thought he must have been slipping away and hearing voices as the Devil took him. But the voice came again, and louder. It was Uncle Harlan calling from down the hillside. Andy managed to shout once, "We're here! We're here, Uncle Harlan!" just as he was lifted off the ground and engulfed into the blackness of the flowing shroud. Smothered in darkness, he could hear Uncle Harlan's muffled voice, "Andy, we're coming." Then, my mother's voice echoed above Uncle Harlan's. "Andrew, it's all right, dear. We're here!" And he was sure now that I had been brought to Hades and was hearing voices from my past.

Suddenly, there was an opening of light and he felt the cool wind on my face again. he saw his mother rush to Mikey and wrap her arms around him while Uncle Harlan bolted toward the black shroud-like a charging bull, his massive body hit the specter low and it tumbled to the ground, releasing its grip on Andy. Andy scrambled behind a tree and watched Uncle Harlan battle with the Devil. They rolled around on the damp ground until the shroud seemed to float above Uncle Harlan, it's long fingers squeezing its talons into his neck. He could see uncle's face turn purple-red as he struggled to free himself, but Andy knew the Devil had the power and Uncle Harlan couldn't save himself or us.

Andy fought off the urge to run to his mother, but instead, moved slowly and cautiously closer to Uncle Harlan with his pocketknife in hand. When Andy was close enough to smell the stench of evil, the Devil carries about him, the Devil suddenly released his hold on his uncle reared up and turned to Andy. Cold fear congealed into icy terror as he beheld those watery red eyes and pointed teeth moving menacingly closer. The talons reached out quickly again, pressing themselves against his throat. He struggled as the Devil's face came close, his foul breath beating against his face, discharge spilling over his thick black lips as they stretched into a sardonic smile. And then, he saw Father Corrigan's face appear over the Devil's like a Halloween mask and the Father said: "Beware the willow wood," before the face dissolved back into the ugliness as quickly as it had appeared.

Andy took a deep breath and held it; raised his arm above his head and brought his knife down, plunging it into the black cloth. The Devil's body jerked once then tumbled backward to the ground, taking the knife with it. Andy watched the dark figure before him as the demonic face melted back into the gentle face of Father Corrigan, with lifeless eyes staring up through the limbs of the willow trees…still now in the calming wind.

Uncle Harlan rushed to Andy; fell to his knees and wrapped him in his arms. Squeezing his eyes shut. Andy buried his face in his uncle's chest, grateful for his comfort and strength.

"It's okay, son," Uncle Harlan assured Andy. "It's over now."

But Andy wasn't sure as he peeked over his uncle's broad back, just enough to see the black robe and the crimson stream bubbling out of the knife wound below the left shoulder, as it ran down over the stitching of the gold crucifix.

Ridley's Rat

Everyone in Lambert County thought Carl Ridley was crazy for keeping a rat as a pet. Some folks were downright angry about it; most were concerned. The last thing a farming community needed was a rat foraging among its livestock and crops. It was bad enough that farm owners had to contend with indigenous predators, but as Sheriff Malcolm said, "To cultivate one and keep it as a pet is a creepy thing."

There had been occasions when a farmer had discovered a portion of his crops eaten or came upon a dead calf lying in an open field partially devoured from its hooves upward. These occurrences had always been attributed to local predators and had been accepted and even expected. But now, if such destruction occurred, Ridley's rat immediately came to mind. Everyone agreed something had to be done. They didn't care that Carl claimed he had never let the rat off his property. It didn't matter to them that he said he kept it in a cage in his barn, letting it out only to walk it on a leash about his grounds, "to give it exercise." As far as they were concerned, the rat had to go.

"Why don't you get yourself an old' tomcat to play with?" Burt Hagger suggested to Carl one night when they were at the bar at the Blue Bonnet Inn. "Or a hound dog to sit with you on your front porch."

Carl spoke over his glass without looking at Burt, his elbows resting comfortably on the bar. He was well kept for sixty, despite years of outdoor farm labor that tanned and wrinkled his skin.

Ridley's Rat

His once dark beard was peppered now with silver-gray, as was his hair, which he kept covered by the New York Mets ball cap he wore, with no allegiance to the team, but merely out of habit.

"Because a cat won't pay you no mind," Carl said. "And a hound dog'll lie in the sun all day, too dumb or lazy to move his ass to the shade. Besides, rats are smart. I read up on it. You can teach them almost anything."

"Like what," Burt Hagger joked, "How to fetch your slippers?"

Carl downed the rest of his beer, turned on his stool, and left Burt Hagger laughing at his own joke.

At the next town council meeting, it was agreed that Sheriff Malcolm would visit Carl Ridley. He would go, not only in his official capacity but also as a friend, to try to persuade Carl to get rid of the rat.

When the sheriff drove the cruiser out to the Ridley farm the following afternoon, things really got weird.

He parked in front of Carl's house, got out and climbed the stairs to the front porch. He rapped on the front door and waited. When no one answered, he shouted Carl's name several times. When there was still no response he walked to the barn expecting to find Carl there. Inside the barn, he let his eyes adjust to the semidarkness, then looked around. He didn't see Carl and supposed he had gone to town for supplies. He would try again tomorrow, but as he turned to leave, someone spoke in a low voice in a far corner of the barn. He listened and walked in the direction of the voice. As he got nearer, he saw Carl Ridley standing in the shadows speaking to someone, and although he couldn't make out the words, Carl's voice was calm and clear, almost instructive, as if he were reciting a lesson, yet the sheriff saw no one other than Carl. Inquisitively, the sheriff moved closer for a better look. He stopped behind Carl's old tractor and leaned his head around the front fender, and that's when he saw it.

Carl Ridley was talking to his rat!

Ridley's Rat

At first, he thought the shadows might be playing tricks on him, but the reality of what he was seeing sent a prickly chill up his spine. In the sallow light streaming through the dirty barn window, Ridley's rat was seated on its haunches on a worktable in front of Carl, its arms outstretched like a child enthusiastically waiting for Carl to feed it the piece of Cornbread Carl had torn from the loaf he held under his arm. After Carl placed the piece of bread on the table, the animal undoubtedly recognized that it was not to accept the bread until Carl gave the verbal command to do so. Upon Carl's command, "Go," it quickly snatched up the bread with its clawed paw and stuffed it greedily into its mouth. Carl broke off another piece from the loaf and placed it on the same spot on the table. This time the animal slapped its paws together in eager anticipation but waited for Carl's instructions once again before taking the piece. Carl laughed hardily, "Very good," he said as he stroked the animal's back in a gesture of approval.

The sheriff stood stunned with disbelief. He was witnessing an exercise in learning, unheard of in the annals of human and animal relations. The rat was interacting with Carl. It, no doubt, understood exactly what Carl expected of it. How could Carl have accomplished such a task? What else might have Carl taught it?

The sheriff watched Carl place the loaf on the floor between his legs and slide a mouth organ out of the top pocket of his bib overalls. Delicately, he tapped the instrument a few times on his thigh, wet his lips, sucked in a lungful of air and began to play an up-tempo of, "Sweet Betsy From Pike." The sheriff's eyes widened. It was impossible, a manifestation of his mind brought on by the summer heat or a lack of sleep. The eeriness of what he was seeing made him uneasy, but he was unable to avert his eyes as he watched Ridley's rat raise itself onto its hind legs and begin to dance happily like a marionette without strings. It kicked its legs and spun about while Carl stomped his foot in time with the music. The sheriff squeezed his eyes shut in an attempt to dispel what he believed could only be an illusion, but when he opened them, the song and dance continued with more exuberance than when it had begun.

The sheriff quickly gave up the idea of seeing Carl that day and crept out of the barn without Carl having ever known he had been there. He never told anyone about what he'd witnessed that afternoon in Carl Ridley's barn, for fear they would deem him mentally unfit to keep his position. But at the next council meeting, the sheriff confessed he had seen the rat once while visiting the Ridley farm, and—at the urging of Mayor Albright—obligingly gave an accurate description of the animal to the committee members.

"It's a big rat," the sheriff began, "bigger than some cats, a four-pounder I'd guess, and not pleasant to look at—not that rats are. Its fur is a dull gray, but for the area around its eyes, which appears darker. Its snout sticks way out and is tipped with a shiny black nose to which wiry whiskers are attached. A set of pointed teeth protrudes from a pair of thick lips that quiver and constantly drip bubbling saliva, giving it the countenance of a vicious predator, which it might well be. Its round fleshy tail is hairless and pink and almost as long as its body. But it's the eyes that give it its most ferocious appearance. They're dark and deep and appear sightless until struck by light when they turn a bloodshot crimson."

"Why does he keep such a hideous thing?" Mayor Albright wanted to know. "It's not something you can love and cuddle."

"It's morbid and strange," Bob Woodman said.

"It might be carrying disease," Bill Smith said. "It could start an epidemic right here in our town. If that thing should bite someone—"

"I share everyone's concerns," Allan Briskly, the town attorney, said. "But we have no legal recourse to compel him to do away with the animal. Just because something *might* happen doesn't give us the right to legally intercede."

"You mean we have to let him keep that thing?"

"Until the animal becomes a danger or a nuisance to the community, there's nothing we can do."

"Well, I know what I can do," Bill Smith said. "Keep my shotgun loaded and by my front door."

"Keep your pants on, Bill," Sheriff Malcolm said. "We might be making too big a thing out of this."

"It's a delicate situation," Allan Briskly said. "It's not like Carl is or has ever been a criminal. We have to treat this carefully."

Mayor Albright shook his head in bewilderment. "Why would anyone want to care for a thing like that? It's not something I'd expect of Carl."

"Carl hasn't been himself since the loss of his daughter," Bob Woodman said. "He's been quiet and reclusive and sometimes downright unfriendly."

"That's understandable," Allan Briskly said. "But it has no relevance to what we're concerned with here. Until some law has been broken, our hands are tied."

Carl and his wife, Ellie, had been solid members of the community for nearly thirty years, and although Carl hadn't been as socially active as he had been before Ellie died, two years ago, he was still respected in the community for the civil work he and Ellie had done during their more youthful years The council members all agreed, a man like Carl Ridley was hard to reproach for an odd but seemingly harmless thing like keeping a rat for a pet. Especially since his only daughter had been murdered just a month earlier. They had seen the changes it made in Carl, his sudden reclusiveness, his unsociability and his desire to be left alone and grieve in his own way. The committee agreed that placing any undue hardship on him now just wouldn't be right.

When Carl returned from the feed store that afternoon on the day of his daughter's murder, he found his daughter lying in the grass by the open doors of the barn. The bruises on her throat made it evident that she had been strangled. The county coroner concurred.

"I know who did it," Carl had told Sheriff Malcolm. "It was that Kirk Mosby. He had it *in* for Melanie ever since she broke it off with him."

"How can you be sure?" the sheriff said.

"Because Melanie told me," Carl said. "When I found her and lifted her into my arms. She whispered Kirk Mosby's name, just before she…"

Emotion prevented the rest of the words from leaving Carl's mouth. He removed a handkerchief from his back pocket and touched it to his moist eyes.

The sheriff put a consoling hand on Carl's shoulder. "Why would Mosby do that if he loved your daughter Carl?"

"Jealousy and rejection," Carl said, "Jealousy and rejection can bring out the rage in a man he never knew he had. Besides, I always thought Kirk was a little *off,* capable of doing such a thing. You know how he was before he met Melanie. I was glad when Melanie stopped seeing him."

"Melanie loved Kirk," the sheriff said. "Maybe she was calling his name as an affirmation of her love for him."

"No," Carl Ridley said. "She was telling me who her killer was."

When the sheriff questioned Mosby, he had an airtight alibi. He claimed he'd been at the Blue Bonnet Inn that afternoon and had procured two drinking buddies willing to testify that they were with him at the time the murder was committed. Their claims generated more ambiguity in the sheriff's mind, but not enough to eliminate Mosby as a suspect. Although he agreed that Carl Ridley's theory of jealousy and rage was a distinct possibility, the sheriff was left with the arduous task of trying to convince Carl that he might be wrong. Carl made it no secret that he believed Kirk Mosby had killed his daughter. He was as adamant about it as he was about keeping his rat.

***

Ridley's Rat

Twenty-five-year-old Kirk Mosby lived with his widowed mother in a small house on the outskirts of town. Kirk had always been somewhat detached, and not very well-liked by the community. He had gotten into trouble more than once with the local law, mostly for minor infractions: drunk and disorderly, public indecency, and had once been arrested for his alleged involvement in a service station hold up for which charges were dropped. Until now Kirk Mosby had a meagerly impressive list of misdemeanors, but now, the bar had been raised by adding the suspicion of murder to that list. He may have wantonly killed the one thing he loved—Melanie Ridley.

Kirk and Melanie met at the 4H club Harvest Dance. They hit it off quickly and ostensibly fell in love. For the next eight months, they were *the couple*. Everyone in the community was aware of their romance. And, in time, Kirk's "bad boy" reputation seemed to fade away in light of his association with Melanie Ridley.

There was nothing inordinate about Kirk and Melanie's relationship, they were young, happy and in love, and even made plans for their future together, until that afternoon outside the barn on the Ridley farm when their plans were shattered.

It had been almost a month since the incident with Melanie, and other than the sheriff questioning Kirk Mosby about it, there had been no further inquiries. Kirk had no fear of being caught. No one could pin it on him. He had left no clue, no evidence that would lead to him. It all happened quickly. She just wouldn't listen. He was sure she still loved him. He had to make her understand that they were meant for each other. Bound by love for eternity. Things had been okay between them until she started acting differently until she told him she didn't want to be tied down and wanted to see other guys. He had begged her, pleaded with her to reconsider.

They had been having a civil discussion on the front porch of the house when she suddenly became annoyed with something he had said. She had asked him to leave, said she never wanted

Ridley's Rat

to see him again. When she stepped off the porch and headed for the barn in an attempt to get away from him. He followed her, and that's when the real arguing began, the arguing and the shouting that led to her slapping him hard across his face, unleashing the anger, frustration, and rage that had been building inside him for weeks. He tried to make her stop hitting him but she wouldn't, until his hands came up around her neck, almost uncontrollably, like they had a life of their own. Wild-eyed, he watched his fingers dig deep into the soft white flesh of her neck. She tried to scream once as he tightened his grip and held her firm while she thrashed about in his grasp like a rag doll. In a few seconds, it was over. He let her lifeless body drop to the ground with no regret, no feeling of guilt or contrition. She deserved what she got. He had given her his heart, and she had shattered it without regard. If she hadn't slapped him, the whole thing might not have happened. But she kept swinging at him and he had to put his arms up to protect his face, especially when she began to scratch and claw at him so fiercely that she yanked off his bracelet.

The bracelet!

He felt a sensation of panic as he suddenly remembered. Yes, he'd been wearing the bracelet, the one she had given him that had his initials engraved on it. He remembered putting it on before going to see her. It had fallen to the ground during the struggle, but he had forgotten about it until just now. It was probably still lying in the grass. If they should search the area and find it, or if old man Ridley should stumble upon it, it would become his one-way ticket to the hangman. But if it had been discovered, the sheriff would have confronted him with it. He had to be sure. He had to go back. He had to find it before someone else did.

***

It was nearly midnight when he parked his car on Emory Road and sprinted across the open field toward Carl Ridley's barn. The moon was full in a cloudless sky, which didn't present the ideal situation for someone trying to go unnoticed, but then, it would illuminate the ground area, making it easier for him to find the bracelet, he thought.

When he reached the barn, he pressed himself against the dark side of the building. He looked back at the house. No lights. Carl Ridley had already gone to bed. It encouraged him to begin searching the spot where he had left Melanie's body. He had followed Melanie from the front porch of the house to the barn where she began her physical assault on him, where; he remembered he had lost the bracelet. The barn doors were open, as usual, and he was sure this was the right place to look. He got on his hands and knees and began sweeping his opened hand across the grass. The grass was wet and cold and his hands and knees quickly became saturated. He wiped his hands several times on his jeans before continuing. He crawled in a circle around the area, feeling every blade of grass and every stone. but his effort only brought him a handful of wet grass and moist soil. He tried circling in the opposite direction, widening his search, this time using both hands to cover more area in a shorter time, but after two full circles, he still came up with nothing. He got to his feet and looked over the area again. Could he be looking in the wrong place? No. He was sure this was where the bracelet fell. It had to be here. He looked up at the house again…quiet, still and dark.

He was about to get down on his knees a second time when he heard the voice behind him from inside the barn. He turned quickly and peered through the open doors into the darkened barn. There stood Carl Ridley, bathed in silver moonlight, like a ghost that had appeared from nowhere, In the crook of his right arm he held a shotgun, its two barrels aimed straight at Kirk Mosby.

"Looking for this?" Carl said as he held up the telltale bracelet in his left hand for Mosby to see. The moonlight bounced off the silver finish as Mosby stared at it with disbelief. It had happened. Carl Ridley had found the bracelet.

"You left your calling card in the grass by the barn," Carl said. "Lucky for me, I found it before the police arrived, and unlucky for you."

It was, of course, Mosby's death warrant.

"Step inside," Carl Ridley said.

Kirk Mosby had no choice but to walk through the barn doors, followed by Carl Ridley and his double barrels.

"All the way to the back wall," Carl said.

Mosby walked to the back wall of the barn, then turned to face Ridley. "Are you going to shoot me?" he said.

"No," Carl said. "Although I could. You're a trespasser." He tossed the bracelet at Mosby. It landed on the floor at his feet.

"She gave that to you with her love," Carl said. "A love that you killed."

"But I didn't kill her," Mosby said. "I came here tonight to find out who did and why. I want to know the truth."

"We'll know the truth before we leave here tonight," Carl said. With this, he turned and looked into the shadows to his left. "Come," he said.

"What did you say?" Mosby said. "I thought you—" But the rest of his words were caught in the tightness of his throat and hung there in his open mouth when he saw the rat. It waddled out of the darkness at Carl Ridley's command and stopped by his feet.

It squatted on its hindquarters, staring intently at Mosby through black hollows that might have been eyes. It bared its teeth several times, spilling syrupy saliva onto the barn floor, making muted squealing sounds while its body quivered as if in a state of anxious agitation. It sat beside Carl like an obedient dog awaiting its next command. Carl looked down at it with an air of parental pride, smiled as he gently stroked its nape, then looked back at Mosby.

"I know you killed my Melanie," he said. "Tell me you did."

"I-I didn't," Mosby said, never taking his eyes off the rat. "I already told you I didn't."

Ridley's Rat

"I'll ask you one more time," Carl said.

"What do you want me to say?" Mosby said.

Without hesitation, Carl looked down at his rat and said, "Go."

The rat dropped forward onto all fours and began a slow walk toward Mosby.

"No! Keep it away!" Mosby shouted. Instinctively, he pressed himself against the wall of the barn.

"Tell me what you did!" Carl said.

"Don't let that thing near me," Mosby shouted. His entire body was trembling now as fear began to build in him. When he took two steps to his right, Ridley's rat took two steps with him...and then one step closer.

"I'll kill it if it comes nearer," Mosby said. But he had no intention of touching the filthy thing, and he had nothing to use as a weapon. If he could run around the rat and out the barn doors, he might be able to outrun it, but then there was Carl Ridley and his shotgun.

In a futile attempt at escape, he turned and ran left toward the far corner of the barn. The rat scurried along with him, making high-pitched squealing sounds as if overjoyed by the thrill of the chase. When Mosby stopped running, the rat stopped with him...and then took another step closer.

Mosby's breathing came hard and fast, his face pale, perspiration dripping into his eyes from his glistening forehead. He squeezed his eyes shut only for an instant and wiped them quickly as he watched the rat lower its head to the ground and begin to stalk toward him. Slowly...calculating...its teeth chattering with excited eagerness, waiting for the right moment to strike.

Images flashed through Mosby's terrified mind as he envisioned the rat gnawing through to the bone of his ankle and then moving quickly up his leg where the flesh was thicker and more succulent. He could feel its coarse fur and rubbery tail against his skin as the animal thrashed about in a feast of frenzy, its razor-sharp teeth ripping flesh and muscle from his vulnerable body. The pain would become unbearable. He heard himself scream, a scream that begged for a swift and merciful death as he fell helplessly to the ground where the beast would make a meal of him until it had its full.

But then he heard Carl give the command; "Quit," and the rat immediately sat back on its haunches and waited like a submissive servant. Carl smiled at the animal, and then looked up at Mosby. "Are you ready to tell the truth?" he said. "Are you ready for a confession?"

"But I already told you, I didn't kill her."

"Lies!" Carl Ridley said and then he gave the command, "Go." The rat lowered itself to all fours again and moved quickly toward Mosby. This time its ferocity was more evident than before as it screeched a loud high-pitched cry that echoed in the hollow ceiling of the barn. It charged Mosby with its mouth wide open; its jagged teeth wet and shining with saliva, in anticipation of its imminent kill.

Mosby screamed and ran on shaky legs until he reached the opposite corner of the barn. The rat stayed close, snapping its jaws at the air near Mosby's heels, squealing and screeching in excited eagerness. Mosby dug himself into the dark corner, knowing it was a false refuge, but desperate for escape. His breathing was labored, and his heart pounded heavily in his chest. The animal was upon him now, no more than three feet away, close enough for him to detect the foul stench it carried with it. Mosby watched in terror as the rat raised itself onto its hindquarters and prepared to spring, its red eyes glowing with excitement, its jaws quivering in avarice anticipation of its reward.

"Call it off!" Mosby shouted. "I admit the murder. I killed her!" Those were his final words before the barn swirled around him in a vortex of light and dark. He grabbed his chest, heaved one last breath, and then collapsed to the floor.

A single gunshot rang out, reverberating against the barn walls and echoing inside the vaulted ceiling. Ridley's rat leaped a foot into the air, spun around one full turn, and then dropped to the floor. It convulsed and kicked for nearly a half-minute before lying motionless.

From behind the old tractor, Sheriff Malcolm emerged, his service revolver still in his hand. Ridley looked angry and surprised as the sheriff approached, looked down at the dead rat and then walked over to Mosby lying in the corner. He bent over him, felt for a pulse and listened for a heartbeat. There was none.

"Why'd you do that? Carl said, more concerned for the loss of his rat than a dead Kirk Mosby.

"Because it had to be done," the sheriff said, "for your sake."

The sheriff holstered his weapon and walked back to where Carl was standing. He eased the shotgun from Carl's arm and set it against an upright behind him.

"How long have you been here?" Carl said.

"Since you came into the barn with Mosby. I followed him here tonight. And it's a good thing I did."

"Why?"

"Because there's a dead man in your barn, Carl. You'll have to account for it."

"But you saw what happened," Carl said. "I didn't kill him. You know that. You heard what he said. He admitted murdering my daughter."

"I heard it," the sheriff said. "But do you think anyone would believe me if I told them what I witnessed here tonight? I'd lose my position, maybe be ordered to undergo a psychiatric evaluation myself. I've got two more years before I retire, Carl."

"But I didn't kill him."

"Yes you did, Carl. The twisted, unbelievable thing you created caused his death. Just as Dr. Frankenstein was responsible for the deaths his creation caused."

"I didn't kill him," Carl repeated. "His heart gave out. You saw it" He tapped his own chest with his finger and said, "Bad ticker."

"How would you know that?"

"Melanie told me. It was a secret the three of us kept."

"Then you knew when you planned this? You knew his heart would..."

"He killed my Melanie," Carl said softly.

The sheriff sat on a small barrel and rubbed his temples between his thumb and forefinger. "This whole thing is fantastic," he said. "No one will believe it." He looked back up at Carl. "But you took a man's life, Carl, and you *should* pay for it."

"Are you gonna arrest me?"

"Not before I take time to think. Put together a plausible story that's as close to the truth as I can make it without compromising my integrity. I've got twenty-three years on the job. I don't want to screw up my retirement pension. We've been friends for a long time, Carl. But tonight, you've put me in a pickle."

***

"Carl Ridley phoned me after midnight," Sheriff Malcolm said. "He told me he had Kirk Mosby corralled in his barn and was holding him at gunpoint till I came to get him. When I arrived, I found Mosby lying on the floor, dead."

The sheriff was addressing Mayor Albright in his office the morning following the incident. Allan Briskly, the town attorney, was also there at the mayor's request. The mayor wanted to know details, and the sheriff was telling the story he had rehearsed over and over in his head, trying to strike a balance between his own moralities and bending the truth enough to keep himself out of harm's way. He had never considered himself a liar, but he wasn't a moralist either. The only lies he'd told were the little "white ones" everyone tells now and then. But now he'd been confronted with something different. He had to protect himself. His self-respect was at stake. That and the sense of justice and fairness he had believed in all his adult life. Carl Ridley had committed a crime, and by all things just and holy, he should answer for what he did. But why should *he* pay for Carl Ridley's crime? Why should *he* be entirely truthful and suffer the inevitable consequences?

"How did this happen?" the mayor said.

The sheriff chose his words carefully before he spoke. "We have Carl's Ridley's statement," he said.

The mayor leaned back in his chair, tented his fingers and bounced them against his lips as he took a moment of thought. "Did Carl attack Mosby?" he said. "We all know how he felt about Kirk Mosby."

"I don't think so," the sheriff said. "The autopsy report will help."

"Seems like a strange coincidence that Mosby winds up dead in Carl Ridley's barn," Alan Briskly said. "What was Mosby doing in the barn? Why was Ridley there at that time of night?"

"Carl claims Mosby came to look for a bracelet he lost the night of the alleged murder," the sheriff began, "one with Mosby's initials on it. Carl, not being a good sleeper, saw Mosby from his bedroom window standing outside his barn. It was easy for him to spot Mosby in the full moonlight. After grabbing his shotgun he hurried to investigate, and found Mosby on his hands and knees searching for the bracelet, 'sniffin' like a hound dog,' Carl said."

The door behind the sheriff opened and the sheriff's deputy came in, carrying a manila envelope. He handed it to the sheriff. "Preliminary medical report," he said, then turned and left.

"I'll take that," Allan Briskly said, sliding the envelope from the sheriff's hand. He opened the envelope and began to read the top printed page. After nearly a full minute, he looked up at Mayor Albright. "Kirk Mosby died of cardiac arrest."

The mayor widened his eyes. "A heart attack? How does a healthy twenty-five-year-old suddenly die of a heart attack?

"According to this, Kirk Mosby was living with congenital heart disease. A condition originated from birth. Any undue stress could cause cardiac arrest and possible death."

The mayor considered this, and then said to the sheriff, "Was there any sign of a struggle at the scene?"

"None I could determine," the sheriff said.

"This report says there wasn't a mark on the body," Allan Briskly added. "Not so much as a scratch."

"Are you suggesting there was no crime committed?" the mayor said to him.

"The report corroborates Carl Ridley's statement," the sheriff said. "Carl admitted he and Mosby had words, and eventually a heated argument ensued. During the shouting and arm-waving, Mosby suddenly began to gasp for air, grabbed his chest and fell to the floor. Carl swears he never laid a hand on him."

The mayor leaned back in his chair, tented his fingers again and touched them to his lips once more. In thoughtful silence, he looked at Allan Briskly and then back at the sheriff. No one said a word.

Later that morning Carl Ridley was released without charges. He went back to his farm and buried his rat.

Sheriff Malcolm took an early retirement.

The Callings

The black SUV rolled through the dark woods with its lights off, its tires crunching twigs and dried leaves, breaking the silence of an arid autumn night. The October moon was bright but did little to penetrate the abundance of trees and closely tangled limbs, leaving this part of the woods in virtual darkness. Carl Bellamy had no trouble finding the small clearing, having been here several times during the past month, he was confident he could find his way. He turned off the engine and maneuvered his ample belly out from behind the steering wheel while Allen Finney got out on the other side. The two men stepped into the returning silence and walked to the rear of the vehicle. When Carl raised the liftgate, the interior light flickered on, illuminating the black canvas body bag they had stuffed into the cargo area earlier. Leaving the gate up so the light would spill out onto the immediate area, they lifted the bag out, carried it a short distance and dropped it on the ground beside a freshly dug grave. Carl pushed the bag over the edge with his foot, causing it to fall into the open pit. It landed in the blackness at the bottom with a muffled *thud*. They each pulled a shovel from a mound of loose soil beside the hole and began filling the void. Both worked in silence, quickly and methodically, as if every movement had been rehearsed. Through the dim light, Carl scanned the several nearby holes, which had been dug and refilled earlier in the month. He was satisfied that it was impossible to detect their presence since the autumn breeze had blown twigs and fallen leaves over the disturbed earth so it blended now with nature's own.

When their assigned task was completed, they tossed the shovels into the SUV closed the liftgate and returned to the front seat. Carl switched on the overhead light and removed a clipboard from between the seats. He scanned the list of names until he found the one he was looking for, then, with his pencil, ran a line through it. "No relatives and no questions," he said. He slid the clipboard back between the seats. "Tomorrow we'll call on Silas Gibb, the widower who lives by Schooley's Point. He'll make number eight."

Allen dropped his head back on the headrest and let out a sigh of relief. "How many more for us?" he said.

"Relax," Carl said. "Think of this as your civic duty."

"It's murder!" Allen snapped.

"No more murder than abortion," Carl said.

"It's not the same."

"Sure it is just the opposite end of the life cycle. Besides, you agreed to do your part like the rest of the council members."

"I don't have to like it."

"We went over this at the meetings," Carl reminded. "It's our only solution. Think of your kids…and mine. Think of their future."

Allen shut his eyes and thought about his wife and two young daughters. Their future was the sole reason he had entered into this unholy alliance.

"Well, it's time someone else took a turn," he said.

"Everybody on the council takes their turn until the job is completed," Carl said. "That was the agreement." He switched off the light. The two men sat in the dark silence staring out at the pinpoints of amber light that was the town nestled in the valley below, its slumbering residents unaware that their name might soon be the next penciled off the long list.

***

Silas Gibb sat on his porch, keeping a watchful eye on the young folks passing his front yard on their way home from school. At eighty-six, he was the oldest resident of Pine Valley and he knew these young "whipper-snappers" had little respect for people and property and needed to be watched.

Time had changed many things in Pine Valley, especially the young people. In his day, youngsters respected their elders and their hard-earned property. But this was a new breed; several generations beyond his own, of people he didn't understand... people he feared.

Fear had been spreading throughout Pine Valley on the autumn wind. Silas heard the fantastic yarns of how the elderly in town were disappearing suddenly and without explanation. Although he thought it all "a bunch of craziness", a small part of him shuddered at the possibility of it being a bizarre reality.

He leaned forward in his rocker now and squinted down the road to see Carl Bellamy's SUV stop by his front gate. He watched warily as Carl struggled out from behind the steering wheel and Allen Finney get out on the passenger side. Silas recalled Allen Finney was the town attorney and Carl a local physician and wondered why they were calling on him today since he had never had much of an acquaintance with either man. As far as he was concerned, they were newcomers to Pine Valley, the "Yuppie" type who bought their way onto the town council for their own advantage.

Carl opened the front gate and the two men walked up the stone path. "Afternoon Silas," Carl said, resting one foot on the porch step and leaning an elbow on the stair rail.

Allen Finney flopped down on the bottom step, removed a handkerchief from his back pocket and began wiping the glisten from the top of his shaved head. "Hot for October," he said.

"Can't spare any water," Silas said, "but got plenty of cold beer."

"We're okay," Carl said. "Just calling to see how folks around here are doing during the...should I say, crises."

The Callings

Silas leaned back in his rocker and ran his arms through his suspenders so they would hang loosely by his sides. "Spend most time these days keeping an eye on young'uns," he said. "Town's overrun with 'em."

"People come here from all over to start families," Carl said.

"We're a growing community," Allen said.

"Growing too fast," Silas continued. "Seems like we're running out of things. Last week the council voted to ration drinking water."

"Only temporary," Carl said.

"What will they take from us next?" Silas said.

"The country's overcrowded," Carl agreed. "The government won't listen to the people and hasn't done anything to alleviate the problem."

"That's why the town council came up with a solution," Allen added. "If the government won't help, people everywhere are fixing the problem in their own way."

"Folks should go back to where they came from," Silas suggested. "And take them young'uns with them."

"There's no place to go back to," Carl offered. " There are just too many people everywhere."

"Been here all my life," Silas said, "always plenty for everybody." He leaned forward in his rocker to make sure the two men heard what he had to say next. "And what about these folks disappearing'?"

There were several moments of silence while Allen waited for Carl to explain.

"Silly rumors," Carl finally said.

Silas looked at him skeptically. "It's the old folks," he reminded.

Carl wiped his forehead with the back of his hand. "Maybe we'll have them beers," he said in an attempt to change the subject.

Silas pushed himself up from his rocker and ran his arms through his suspenders, snapping them back onto his shoulders. He turned toward the house, pulled back the screen door and walked gingerly toward the kitchen.

Carl climbed the steps quickly, motioning for Allen to follow. They took a position on either side of the door. Carl pulled a leather case from his pocket and removed a syringe that had been filled with a clear liquid. He held it in the ready position with his thumb on the plunger and waited.

They could hear Silas through the screen, rattling utensils, slamming drawers and grumbling about not being able to find a bottle opener. In a short while, he appeared back at the door, balancing an armful of beer bottles. Pushing the screen back, he stepped out onto the porch. Before the door closed—they were on him!

***

"We have a problem," Mayor Carmichael said, opening his spiral-bound notebook.

Allen Finny sat at the long mahogany table with the other council members and waited to hear the news. He wondered how long it would take their "perfect plan" to go awry. He had been struggling for more than a month with the morality of *"mandatory defoliation of elderly citizens,"* since reluctantly agreeing with the council to implement the plan.

In addition to Carl and himself, the council included: Mayor Carmichael, Police Chief Kaminski and Tom Reagan the town benefactor who had once been mayor.

"Subject number eight," the mayor continued, sliding his finger down the list of names and dates. "Mr. Silas Gibb. I believe that was your assignment, Carl."

"Mine and Allen's," Carl said.

"Despite the council's extensive research in compiling the subject list," Tom Reagan said, "an unexpected relative has surfaced and is enquiring as to Mr. Gibb's whereabouts."

"I was assured every detail was accounted for," Allen said.

"Contingencies," Tom Reagan added. "We were aware that something like this could happen but didn't think it would. We were all very thorough, Allen."

"Who is it?" Carl said.

"I can explain," a voice echoed from the far end of the table. Police Chief Kaminski pushed his huge body up from his armchair and stood before the council. He was a big man with broad shoulders and biceps as thick as his thighs. He placed his lit cigar in the ashtray on the table and wiped his lips with the back of his hand before he spoke.

"A young woman came to my office two days ago looking for her uncle, the aforementioned Mr. Gibb. She explained that she had been attending school in Europe and since the unexpected death of her parents in an auto accident; Mr. Gibb had become her only living relative. She wrote to him last month, and they made arrangements for her to come to Pine Valley. When she arrived at the address he'd given her—"

"She found the place empty, of course," Allen interjected.

"It seemed odd to her that he wasn't there since he knew when she was to arrive. Considering his age, she concluded he couldn't have gone far and decided to spend the night. When there was no sign of him in the morning, she came to me."

"How did you handle it?" Carl said.

"I wasn't sure if he was on the list, so I drove her back to the place and gave it a good looking over. Under the circumstance, there wasn't a plausible explanation to give her. I told her I'd follow up and call her when I found anything. She assured me she'd be staying at the house until her uncle showed up."

"Has she filed a missing person's report?" Allen said. "We don't want the county involved in this."

"No—but this girl wants answers," the chief said. He retrieved his cigar from the ashtray and eased back into his armchair, losing himself in the pleasure of a long draw and the aromatic smoke that encircled his head.

"What do you propose to do?" the mayor asked Allen.

Allen threw an incredulous look at Carl, then back at the mayor. "I don't see why we—"

"The assignment belonged to both of you," the mayor interrupted. "We can't continue the program until this problem is resolved."

Allen stood quickly. "But it's our problem," he said. "Each one of us. We're all in this together."

"It was your assignment," the mayor reminded.

"And your responsibility to make it right," Tom Reagan added.

The Mayor stood and closed his notebook. "I'll expect results by our next council meeting on Tuesday," he said. "Do what you have to do."

***

"I'm glad you agreed to come with us," Carl said to the chief. "The uniform will make things more official and your size is an intimidating factor."

They were in Carl's SUV on their way to the Gibb home.

"Why does his size matter," Allen asked, "if we're just trying to convince this girl that we're going to locate her uncle?"

"In case we're not convincing enough," Carl said. He turned the SUV off the main road and stopped by the front gate of the Gibb house.

"Let the chief do most of the talking," Allen suggested. "We don't want this to get out of hand."

They climbed the steps to the porch, and the chief rapped on the screen door. When the door opened, Allen peered around the chief's broad shoulder to see a woman in her mid-twenties with short black hair, dressed in shorts and a sweatshirt.

"These men are from the council," the chief said.

She led them to a front room where they sat on a well-worn sofa. The woman stood before them with her hands on her hips, her muscular legs twitching nervously while she waited for some news. Allen couldn't help thinking she looked like a "butch" drill sergeant.

"We're here to assure you we're doing everything we can to find your uncle," the chief said. "His disappearance is disturbing to all of us."

The Callings

"He's the only relative I have now," the girl said. She spoke not with sorrow but with a kind of anger as if the only thing she had in the world had been unjustly taken from her. "Shouldn't you have something by now?"

"We're utilizing every channel," the chief said.

"Seems to me the longer he's missing, the harder he'll be to find."

"These things take time."

The girl walked to a portable bar by the front window and poured herself a glass of water from a pitcher. She didn't offer any. "When I call your office, they tell me the same thing."

"We're a small department," the chief said.

"I don't think your people could find a full moon on a dark night," she said. She took a long drink, then set the glass down. "I've decided to notify the county and file a missing person's report."

"That's not the smart thing to do," Carl said. He stood and walked closer to the girl. "We need more time."

"You've had enough time."

"It will only complicate things if you do this," Carl continued.

"I'm sure we'll have something in a few days," the chief added.

"The county will do a better job," the girl said.

Allen saw the chief throw a furtive look at Carl, then get up from the sofa and walk behind the girl.

"It's your job to find him, not mine," she was saying to Carl. "If you hadn't taken—"

The rest of her words were lost to an inarticulate muffle as the chief's big hand came down over her mouth. He swung his free arm quickly around her waist, locking her arms at her sides, leaving her helpless in his massive grip.

Allen jumped up and approached Carl. "This is wrong!" he shouted.

Carl removed the leather case from his pocket and lifted out the liquid-filled syringe.

"It was supposed to be only the elderly," Allen reminded, "to make room for everyone else."

"She's leaving us no choice," Carl said, positioning his thumb on the plunger.

The girl squirmed and kicked to free herself as Carl started toward her with the syringe. Allen moved quickly, knocking Carl against a wall while trying to snatch the syringe from his hand. But Carl was quicker. He pushed Allen away with his free arm, keeping the syringe in the air above his head out of harm's way. Allen charged him a second time, but now Carl brought his hand up to meet Allen's throat, pressing his thumb against his windpipe. Allen tugged at Carl's fingers, struggling for air, his eyes wide, his face turning purple-red, but Carl squeezed harder pressing his thumb deeper into the cavity and keeping it there until Allen sunk slowly to his knees as helpless as the girl, his mouth widening to a silent scream as he collapsed to the carpeted floor.

***

The SUV crunched its way through the dark woods, stopping at the small clearing. Carl and Chief Kaminski got out and removed the two bodies from the rear, carried them to an open grave and dropped them to the bottom. Without hesitation, they began shoveling soil into the hole.

"We'll update the council members at the meeting tomorrow," Carl said. "The girl won't be missed, but this Allen thing will have to be dealt with."

Only their labored breathing and the sound of moist earth hitting the bottom of the black hole broke the silence. When the work was nearly completed, the chief paused to wipe his forehead with the back of his hand. "Allen just couldn't understand that we're doing the right thing," he said. "Just trying to make things better for everyone's future."

"It's only the natural progression of things," Carl agreed, tossing the last shovelful of soil onto the grave. "Out with the old, in with the new."

The Men of Salem County

Contrary to popular belief, a man can be a witch. Such was the case with Arlen Hightower. All the men of Salem County knew Arlen was a witch. They were sure of it.

One afternoon Carl Hicks climbed into the back of Joe Morgan's pickup truck with the other men and rode out to Arlen's place. Carl was a bit shaky. This was the first time he had ever done anything like this. The men at the barbershop had been talking about Arlen for several months and when they decided it was time to do something, Carl agreed to go along. They had done the same thing to Harley Brenner two years ago, but Carl chose to stay out of it then. Now, he believed it was the right thing to do.

Carl had nothing personal against Arlen. He kind of liked him. But Arlen was a fool. Not because of the way he acted, but because of the way he looked. It was Arlen's eyes that gave him away. They reminded Carl of a cat's eyes. The way he looked through those glassy gray pupils was enough to make anybody shiver. And Arlen's hands weren't right, either; there wasn't a callus on them and his fingers were long and slender and each one was tipped with a pointed fingernail. They sure weren't the hands of a farmer. If Arlen had a wife, she might have given him hell about it. Arlen should have paid more attention to his fingernails. Although he lived alone, Arlen was sociable enough and got along with most folks. "That's the way witches are," the men had told Carl. "They disguise themselves so they fit in."

The Men of Salem County

When they got to Arlen's place they found him hiding behind his barn. Arlen claimed he was chasing a fox from his chicken coup, but they knew he was trying to get away from them. Ron Stokley and a few other men chased Arlen around the barn. When they caught him, they tied his wrists and ankles with a length of rope. Arlen fought and shouted as they carried him to the Oaktree in his side yard.

"This is crazy," Arlen said. "You all know me."

"We know what you are," Allan Culpepper said.

"You can't fool us any longer!" Burt Wickers shouted as he tossed Carl a coil of rope. Carl looked at the noose that had been fashioned at one end and hesitated before placing it over Arlen's head. Burt threw the other end of the rope over a large limb and he and Allan Culpepper pulled Arlen up off the ground. Arlen dangled from the rope for a while but didn't die. He just hung there, kicking and jerking for the longest time, until Bill Moses finally cut him down. On the ground, Arlen thrashed about until some men started beating him with their clubs, but he still kept squirming and flopping. So Joe Morgan came up and cut off Arlen's head with his grub axe, and then he cut off his arms, and then his legs. Joe kept swinging his axe until there were only small chunks of Arlen left on the ground; even then, the pieces squirmed and quivered and took a long time to settle down. *Witches are hard to kill*, Carl thought.

They were going to bury the pieces in the woods but Joe Morgan shouted, "Better burn 'em to be sure." Joe got a can of gas from his truck and doused the pieces good. When Roy Hemmer tossed his cigarette into the mess, the whole thing went up quickly. Carl felt queasy as he watched the pieces char and sizzle. After the last of the smoldering pieces died out, he climbed back into Joe Morgan's pickup with the others, and they all went home to supper.

When Carl got home, he went to the kitchen sink to wash. Living alone had its advantages, like choosing what to have for supper without having to consider anyone else. He'd cook himself some potatoes and a slice of beef as soon as he finished washing. He scrubbed his hands with soap and a hand brush, working the lather into his long fingers and being careful to clean the dirt from under his nails. As he washed, he thought about how foolish Arlen Hightower had been. He'd made it easy for the men to discover what he really was. Harley Brenner had made the same mistake and suffered the same fate as Arlen. They should have been more diligent in protecting themselves from the suspecting eyes of the townsfolk. It was important to blend in and be what they expected you to be. Carl dried his hands at the sink and then took a seat at the table. He laid his hands flat on the tabletop and spread his fingers wide to examine them. The nails were always the problem—the potential giveaway. They grew fast and long and always to a fine point; left unattended, they would begin to resemble talons. He took his penknife from his overalls pocket and began carefully trimming each nail back to the fingertip. The men of Salem County were getting good at spotting witches, and he wasn't about to make the same mistake Arlen Hightower had.

Morena's Revenge

With a trembling hand, I put pen to paper, recalling the grisly events that have consigned me to the hangman. I fear, I dread, I torment, as I sit imprisoned within these walls awaiting my fate. A fate unjustly thrust upon me by misfortune. Of sympathy, I expect none. Of understanding, I can merely be hopeful. It is only justice, after I am gone, that I trust these words will deliver. Yet, there is no remorse for the deed, remorse infers guilt, of which I have none. You will see, I am the victim of the occurrence, not the villain.

I had lived with Elisabeth for several years since our marriage. She was a woman of exceptional beauty. I had treasured her from the moment I saw her and knew she was the woman with whom I wanted to spend my life. We married soon after college and lived comfortably in a large stone house, which I was fortunate enough to have inherited from my father's estate. The house was surrounded by acreage and situated within the green hills of the New England countryside. Elisabeth loved its quietude and quaintness, and I looked forward to its solitude after a day's work. Although Elisabeth and I were childless, our love for each other grew with the years and our happiness grew with it…until the day Elisabeth received a telegram from Doctor Gordon.

The good doctor informed Elisabeth that her mother had been injured in a fall and should not be left unattended since she would be convalescing for some time, and—being a widow—had no one to care for her. Naturally, Elisabeth insisted her mother stay with us during her healing process. My relationship with my wife's mother had been a temperate one, with no inordinate emotions between us. Therefore, being the understanding husband I was, I immediately made arrangements to have Morena transported from her hospital bed to our home.

It was on that cursed day my living nightmare began. For soon after Morena's arrival, I felt a marked neglect from Elisabeth. She directed her attention to her mother's well-being to the exclusion of everything, including me. In time, she began to neglect herself as well. The once golden sheen in her hair faded to a lusterless pallor, as did the vibrant color in her cheeks. When I implored her to see her way, she insisted her mother's health was paramount. My efforts to make her see what she was becoming were futile. Resignedly, I let her have her way with the expectation that Morena would recover quickly and leave our home. But she did not. Although her condition improved to the point where she could walk about her room unassisted, Elisabeth insisted her mother remain with us until her recovery was complete. I relented.

Weeks passed, and to abate the tedium of her confinement, Elisabeth brought her mother a sewing kit to help pass her time. This included an abundance of various colored threads, different sized needles and a multitude of patterns from which to create a variety of stitching projects. Morena embraced her new hobby, and in time, became proficient with needle and thread, even to the degree of making new pillow covers for the sitting room sofa.

As for me, my days were insufferable. I found no joy in returning home after work to the place I once cherished. Now, my nights were empty and lonely, while my wife spent her time in the second-floor room attending to her mother's comforts.

As time passed, I took my comfort from the liquor cabinet. I imbibed more than my share and enjoyed it without contrition, wine and whiskey helped me escape the surroundings into which I had been imprisoned. The libation allowed me to see Morena for what she truly was, an insidious old woman whose presence was the destruction of my marriage and my life. Three *was* a crowd and what had begun as an annoyance grew to a loathing for her with each passing day. Morena developed a mutual disgust for me as well, unjustly blaming me for what her daughter had become, accusing me of neglecting my wife and my home and calling me an indolent drunkard.

In time there evolved a discernable change in my wife, as well. Influenced by her mother, she had developed a misguided belief that I was responsible for our happy days being behind us. Oh, the torment and heartache of being abandoned by the woman I loved!

Up to this point, there had been only malicious bickering between Morena and I, until one evening, as we were engaged in a violent shouting match, she stood in the doorway of her room; her face livid, promising vengeance for what she believed I had done to her daughter. "You'll pay for what you've done," she shouted, shaking a clenched fist. "I'll have my revenge!" I took the threat idly and thought no more about it. What had I to fear from a half-crippled aging woman?

I began to spend more time away from home. Each evening, after work, I would visit *The Bird's Nest*, a local tavern where I sat alone and drank away my oppression for hours, returning home only after I was sure Elisabeth and her mother had retired for the night. In the morning, I would leave for work earlier than usual, to avoid their unwarranted bickering. In time, all communication between us ceased. For a long while, my days lingered in this way. My drinking became excessive and soon became a prevailing habit.

One evening, during the third week of my torment, after having stopped by *The Bird's Nest* for my usual aggregate of drink; I chanced upon my old friend, Jacob Corbett. Jacob had been a friend and college classmate whom I hadn't seen in years. We embraced the joy of seeing each other again and took a table together. The evening passed over beer and whiskey and the telling of small lies about our lives. At length, I invited him to my home. An evening of conversation and companionship would be a welcome pleasure for me.

We arrived shortly before midnight. Elisabeth and her mother were long asleep, and the house was dark and quiet. At the sitting-room table, I set up wine and cheese and we drank and ate while we told tall tales about our schooldays. As the night progressed, I suggested a game of Gin Rummy. Jacob agreed, and I retrieved a deck of cards from the breakfront drawer and a fresh bottle of wine. We played and laughed for nearly an hour until Jacob suggested—to abate the monotony—that we place a small wager on the games. I agreed. As the night wore on, our drinking increased, as did our wagers. I had been losing steadily and our game became not a game of enjoyment but a struggle of wits for the large sum of money on the table between us. After more than a dozen hands, I believed I finally held a winning group of cards. When the time came, I cheerfully revealed my hand to my friend. Or should I say, my opponent? He looked surprised as he focused his glassy eyes on the cards spread before him and then at the large pile of cash beside them.

"At last," I said, "it is my turn to collect."

As I reached to gather my winnings, Jacob stood suddenly and pointed a shaky finger at me. "Cheat!" he shouted. "You have not won a single hand all night, and suddenly, you claim the largest prize of all."

I was, at first, taken aback by this accusation. Realizing my friend was heavily intoxicated, I endeavored to explain my winning as honest luck. However, he was obstinate and waved his arms in anger.

"You have brought me here tonight to steal my money," he said. "A clever ruse!"

"You are wrong, my friend," I pleaded. "I have played the game fairly."

When I approached him to calm his concerns, he pushed away from me in the direction of the fireplace. Upon placing my hand on his shoulder, he turned suddenly and grabbed the iron poker from the hearth and swung it in a wide arc in my direction. I was surprised by this turn of events and attributed his rage to the large amount of wine he had consumed. Nonetheless, his mission was to do me bodily harm, and I had no option but to defend myself. I sidestepped the blow, but he raised the iron again, this time bringing it down like a hammer. I reached up and grabbed the iron, and a struggle ensued. He fought like a madman, his eyes ablaze, his face writhing in contortions of indignation. When I secured the iron from his grasp, he charged me like a bull, knocking me against the mantel and bringing his sweaty hands up quickly around my neck. I struggled for air as he pressed his thumbs steadily into my throat. Gasping and choking, I managed to swing the poker against the side of his head. It landed with a *crack*, and Jacob Corbet slid to the floor at my feet.

I paused to regain my breathing and then knelt beside him. The crimson discharge oozing from the wound in his skull caused me to grimace. His sightless eyes staring at the yellowed ceiling and the stillness of his body told me Jacob Corbet was dead.

I took my seat at the table, and with trembling hands, poured myself a glass of wine. In a matter of minutes, my life had gone from bad to worse. I was now accountable for a corpse which was none of my design. The house was quiet. Elisabeth and Morena had, no doubt, slept through the commotion. I collected my thoughts and decided quickly my best course of action was to dispose of the body. A police investigation would not prove favorable to me, and upon learning of this encounter, Morena would delight in trying to convince the authorities I had deliberately committed murder.

I walked back to the corpse and lifted it over my shoulder. Struggling with the burden, I walked through the kitchen and opened the door to the cellar. Carefully, I descended the stone stairs into the darkness. At the bottom, I removed the lantern from the hook where it hung and lit it with a match from my pocket. I made my way through the chilled dampness of a long corridor to the extreme of the cellar, passing neglected rooms that had been of no use to me other than to serve as a repository for a few pieces of old furniture and some rusted garden tools. I secured a spade and bow saw and continued to the smallest room at the most remote end of the corridor. I dropped the corpse to the earth floor and stood in the silence. There were no windows in the room, and a narrow archway entrance kept it obscured from the rest of the cellar.

I placed the lantern on the ground and went to work digging a hole in the loose soil at the center of the floor. I worked until the hole was large enough to contain the remains and then took up the bow saw and kneeled beside the corpse. In my cleverness to conceal the crime, I had determined I must not only hide the cadaver but also dismember it. A dissected corpse would decay more quickly than the whole of its parts.

I began by sawing off the head first, looking away as Jacob Corbet watched me with vacant eyes. Then I sawed off the arms and finally the legs. Being careful not to get blood-spattered, I kicked each member into the hole with my boot. When the torso alone remained, it became necessary to push this heaviest of the body parts over the edge with my hands. With a quick but strenuous effort, it landed at the bottom of the pit with a *thud*. My blood ran cold.

More than an hour passed, and I hastened to make an end to my labor before the sun rose. As I began tossing shovelfuls of earth back into the hole, I was suddenly overcome with the peculiar feeling that I was not alone. Perhaps a feeling of guilt or remorse was playing tricks on me. I stopped and stood motionless, listening for any sounds from the corridor. I retrieved my lantern and scanned the darkness. My light shone through the archway and traveled over the stone and mortar walls, passing glistening webs as eight-legged creatures scrambled for the refuge of darkness. Seeing nothing untoward, I concluded it was a manifestation of my own mind, and returned to the task before me.

When at last, the void was filled; I loosened the top layer of soil to match the soil surrounding it. Satisfied that any recent disturbance of the area was undetectable, I returned the tools, replaced the lantern and climbed the stairs back to the upper floor to retire for the night.

After an uneasy sleep, I awoke the following morning as if from a bad dream. The burden of the previous night's event weighed heavily on my mind. My head was aching, and my body was weak. I bathed and dressed and thought a large breakfast might relieve my anxiety.

On my way to the kitchen, I found Elisabeth and her mother in the sitting room, standing by the opened front door. Elisabeth carried an overnight bag.

"I am taking mother home," she said, "and will be staying with her indefinitely."

I was surprised and dismayed upon hearing this and stepped closer to her with pleading eyes.

"It is no use," she said before I could utter a word. "I can no longer live alone with you."

Morena spoke not a word, but the vengeance in her eyes burned through me like the fires of Hell, revealing more to me than any words she could speak. I could offer no dissent as they entered a cab and I watched it drive away.

I had finally been confronted by the fear I dreaded. Although Elisabeth held feelings of ill will toward me, my compassion for her was unyielding. She had become a misguided and confused wife, prejudiced by a sinister old woman. I could only hope this nightmare would soon end, and my good wife would return to me.

From that night forward, my only companion was the bottle. As I drank, thoughts of Jacob Corbet's withered remains below me swirled in my head. One night as I sat in a half stupor, I saw his decayed and bloated corpse appear at the table opposite me, pointing an accusing finger in my direction. Compelled by fear and anger, I hurled a full bottle of whiskey at the horrific image and it vanished in an instant. It was as though his ghost had risen from the cellar to haunt me. I drank more to obliterate the specter.

Another week passed, and I felt confident the crime would never be discovered. I had been drinking less and thinking more about how to bring my beloved wife home to me and return my marriage to its blissful state.

It was, however, on the following Saturday evening that I received a visit from the local authorities. In my doorway stood a young uniformed policeman and a well-dressed older detective. I allowed them entrance without trepidation.

"We are investigating the disappearance of one Jacob Corbett," the detective said.

"The barkeeper at *The Bird's Nest* identified you as a regular and recalled you and Mr. Corbett drinking there last week. He remembered seeing the two of you leave together."

"The barkeeper is correct," I said. "We had come here for a nightcap, and after a short visit, my friend left for home. I haven't seen him since." My manner was convincing.

The detective thought for a moment and then continued. "There is a second matter, possibly related to the first," he said. "Police headquarters has received a wire, stating there had been heard numerous quarrels from inside this house. The anonymous sender claimed the shouting had been of such magnitude, they believed someone's life might be in peril."

I laughed and assured him that the only persons living with me were my wife and her half invalid mother and that they had been away and I'd been alone in the house for the past week. Here, he produced a warrant to search the premises. This I had not expected, but I cooperated fully, for what had I to fear?

I led them through the rooms on the main floor and guided them through the second-floor bedrooms. They searched well, every closet and corner. When the time came, I advised them to be cautious on the stone stairs as we descended into the cellar. Feeling no anxiety, I removed the lantern from its hook and lighted their way, cordially. They searched like alley cats, every inch of every room, and I was amused by their ineptness and gratified by my own cunning.

At length, we came to the small room at the end of the corridor. The policemen entered before me, and I followed with the light. As I passed beneath the archway, the glaring rays of my light fell upon a vision of overwhelming horror. Had I gone mad? Had I been haunted by a specter of my own making? For a moment, my companions stood motionless, shocked and awed at the scene before them. Overcome by the ghastly presence, I fell back against the opposing wall, dropped the lantern and gave out a long shrill cry, for my fate had been sealed. The light from the lantern bounced along the stonewalls until it came to rest upon the corpse of Jacob Corbet, precariously seated in a far corner upon the earth floor. The rough stitching securing the head and limbs to the torso, and the contrast of black thread against sallow dead skin, revealed one certain conclusion—Morena had procured her revenge!

Dark Places

Mary Jane Kelly pulled her shawl up around her pretty neck against the bitter chill of a mid-November night. The shawl was thin and almost as ragged as the coat she wore. She had promised herself a new coat before the cold weather arrived, but business on the streets had not been good—not since the murders began.

In the past, she could rely on her fine figure and natural good looks to help her eat and pay her bills, but now she was six weeks behind with her room rent, and that "arsehole" landlord was threatening to put her on the street permanently. Typically, she would entertain a customer or two each night, but, like the other girls, she was afraid, afraid of the strangers and the dark places.

Tonight, she was waiting outside The Ten Bells Public House to meet Julia, a new girl who had only recently begun working the streets. Mary and Julia had engaged in a conversation at The Ten Bells the previous night and had become friendly right away. Inevitably, the conversation had turned to money, and the lack of it, when Julia offered to share Mary's room and pay half her rent.

"I need a permanent place," Julia had said, "and paying half rent would save us both a few quid."

Mary had considered it providence and heartily agreed to the offer. As she looked down the empty street, she hoped Julia would show and hadn't changed her mind.

The Ten Bells was a place where the ladies would meet each evening before they went off to work. They'd gossip about each other and discuss the events of the neighborhood. The ritual was more a show of solidarity and a feeling of giving each other some mental solace, especially now that there was danger lurking in every corner of Whitechapel.

Mary recalled the previous night's conversation as she waited.

"The bloke's done in four already," Mollie Jones said.

"Poor Annie Chapman gutted like a fish," Maggie added.

Mary wrapped her arms around herself and shuddered as the image flashed in her mind.

"I think we should walk in pairs," she had suggested. "It's safer."

"Oh, sure," Carly said. "One can provide the service while the other looks on."

The girls had laughed heartily over that silly idea. But the terror of the brutal murders that had been plaguing London's East End remained deep in their hearts.

Mary peered down the street again, straining her eyes through the darkness. To her relief, she saw Julia emerging from the shadows in her direction. Although she and Julia were practically strangers, she was glad to see her and felt certain their newfound relationship would make things financially better for them both.

"Waiting long, dearie?" Julia said as she and Mary stepped into the alcove of The Ten Bells. The lamplight fell over Julia's face and Mary saw now that her new friend looked somewhat older than she had the night before. Although her blonde hair was stylishly stacked high above her head, the lines and wrinkles around her eyes and lips told Mary she had had less than an easy life, and although there was a sensual attractiveness about her, no amount of lip rouge or face powder could conceal her true age. She was wearing a dark waist-length coat with ivory buttons and a Beaver fur collar. It was the kind Mary wanted to buy for herself before street business declined.

"I'm glad you came," Mary said, "I'm anxious to show you the room. Like I said, it's not much, but it's a place to be safe and keep the cold out."

"I'm in no position to be particular," Julia said.

"Should we start straight off?" Mary said. "Or stop inside for a pint?"

"A pint would warm up these bones," Julia said, "But I don't have a penny."

"Nor I," Mary said. "But I'll make a promise to the barman. One I don't intend to keep. He'll give us a pint to share."

They giggled at Mary's mischievous scheme as they went inside and found a table in a corner by the front window. While Julia took a seat, Mary went to the bar, and after a quick whisper in the barman's ear, came back to the table with a pint of gin and two glasses.

The Ten Bells was crowded as usual, with its boisterous laughter and constant dissonance coming from the men at the dartboard. In a far corner near the bar, Alec McMann was playing his music box while several ladies danced atop a pair of tables that had been pushed together. The mantel of smoke that hung in the air made it difficult to see across the room. That's why Mary didn't notice Charlie O'Keefe approaching their table until he slid into the chair beside her and draped his arm over her shoulders. Charlie was drunk, which was his usual condition. He carried a mug of ale balanced delicately in a shaky hand that he sipped from between sentences of slurred words.

"My favorite lady," Charlie said. "How are we tonight?"

"Better, before you got here," Mary said. She removed his smelly arm from around her shoulders and let it drop on the table.

"And who's our friend?" he said. "Never seen ya about, missy."

"She's new," Mary said. "If you must know?"

"A lady of the night," he said. "You'll have no trouble finding blokes in Whitechapel." He leaned closer to Julia and lowered his voice to a whisper. "As long as you don't find ol' leather apron," he added.

Mary knew "leather Apron" was the name the local press had given to the murderer that had been stalking the dark streets and narrow alleys of Whitechapel. Although recently they had been calling him, "The Ripper."

Charlie leaned back in his chair, drained what was left in his mug, let out a short but noxious belch, then wiped his mouth on his grimy coat sleeve before he continued. "A real brute that one is. Down on whores and glad to do away with as many as he can find."

"Clam up, Charlie," Mary said, after seeing the sudden apprehension on Julia's face.

"And hard to catch, he is," Charlie continued, "in and out of the shadows like a wharf rat. Some think he might be a seaman, comes down off a docked ship, does the devil's work then disappears back into the hatches."

"Go fetch another ale," Mary said, "and let us be."

Ignoring Mary's demand, Charlie stood up on unsteady legs, looked about the room furtively, then reached into his coat pocket and brought out a folded seaman's knife. Carefully, he opened the six-inch blade, leaned over the table and held it close in front of Mary and Julia. They could see it had a bone-white handle with a leather lanyard attached to it. The blade was serrated, polished bright and came to an angled point at its end.

"It's a tool like this the bloke would use," Charlie said. "She'll cut through bone and flesh without a workout." As he spoke, he moved the knife about in the air in short circular motions, simulating the ease with which the blade might be employed. Mary watched with growing revulsion as images of the brutal murders flashed across her mind. "And when the work's done," Charlie said, "she's folded and put away neatly—until she goes to work again."

He held the knife motionless now and stared at it almost hypnotically with his watery gray eyes. "I seen Kate Eddowes," he said, "over on Mitre Square, a butcher's work, indeed. Legs spread wide, petticoat up about her waist and her innards lying there on the walkway beside her. To be sure, ladies, it was a sight I never—"

Dark Places

"Stop! Stop!" Mary shouted as she covered her ears with her hands.

Julia jumped up from her chair. "Leave us alone," she said. "Get yourself back to the bar." She pushed Charlie hard on his shoulder, almost knocking him off his feet.

"Okay, okay," Charlie said, "I'm only saying for your own good." He folded his knife and dropped it back into his pocket. As he staggered away, he offered one last admonition, "Keep out of dark places," he said. "Ya might find leather apron, or he might find you."

After Charlie vanished into the smoke, and disorder of The Ten Bells. Julia took her seat again and offered Mary a consoling voice. "What an awful man," she said.

"Charlie's soaked to the gills, as usual," Mary said. "And having a bit of fun at our expense."

"It wasn't fun for me," Julia said.

"Nor I," Mary agreed. "But what he said is true. It makes me shudder."

"Well, let's not think about it,' Julia said. "Let's get to your room. We'll feel better when we get there."

After Mary regained herself and they drained their glasses, they left The Ten Bells and started down Commercial Street toward Miller's Court where Mary had her room. The fall moon was bright but did little to light the dark streets and narrow alleys of Whitechapel. They stayed close as they walked, partly because of the bitter chill the wind carried, but mostly out of a sense of dread.

They continued down Commercial Street until they turned onto Hobson Street. There were no lamps on these side streets and other than an interior glow from an occasional nearby window, the streets were in virtual darkness. They were rounding a bend at the end of the street when Julia felt Mary's hand on her shoulder. Mary pulled her close against the cold brick of a building and stood in cautious silence.

"What is it?" Julia said.

"I see someone," Mary said, looking back into the darkness.

Julia peered into the shadows where Mary was looking. "I don't see anything," she said.

"Along that wooden fence," Mary said, pointing a shaky finger. "The figure of a man with a long coat and hat. He's been following us."

Julia squinted her eyes and looked hard along the fence line but saw nothing.

"Someone's on these streets, no matter what time it is," she said, trying to alleviate Mary's fears and abate her own. "Don't let Charlie O'Keefe get to you, dearie."

Mary gave Julia an incredulous look. "Ain't you afraid of *him*?" she said.

"...of Charlie?"

"No, of *him*," Mary said.

"Sure I am," Julia said, "all the ladies are afraid of *him*." She put a reassuring hand on Mary's shoulder. "Come on, dearie, let's get to your room where it's safe. Is it much further?"

"Not much," Mary said. She looked about one more time before stepping warily off the curb. Her pace was quicker than before as she crossed the cobblestone street.

Julia followed close behind Mary, keeping up her own pace.

At the end of Hobson Street, they came upon the dark silhouette of the old schoolhouse looming against a cloudless sky. Behind the schoolhouse was an open field that had been used as a schoolyard for the children. They had to pass the schoolyard on their way to Dorset Street, which led to Miller's Court. The schoolhouse blocked the light from the moon, keeping the schoolyard in total darkness. They stopped and looked into the vast wasteland of blackness stretching before them, listening to the wind whistling through the weeds and high grass. Neither of them spoke, until Mary said, "There is no other way to go."

"We'll keep on this side of the street," Julia said. "It'll be okay."

They started down Hobson Street again, listening to the wind and the echo of their boot heels on the pavement. As they got closer to the schoolyard, Mary felt the heat of anxiety surge through her body. She gripped her shawl tight about her shoulders, telling herself not to look into the yard, but to keep up a steady pace and continue looking ahead. But even in her fear, she couldn't help darting a look into the black emptiness that was directly across from them now. When she gave a reassuring glance back at Julia, who was several yards behind her, she wondered why Julia wasn't walking faster. Wasn't she afraid?

She was about to urge Julia to pick up her pace when she heard the sound echoing out of the darkness across the street. She listened again and perceived what sounded like heavy boots crunching gravel as if someone were running. She waited and listened again. Someone was running, running hard and fast across the schoolyard.

But why hadn't Julia heard it?

Maybe it was just in her mind. Maybe Charlie O'Keefe had gotten to her. Perhaps it was just her imagination, her fear that was making her see and hear these things, just Charlie O'Keefe's stories still in her head. But no, the running was louder and much closer. She was sure of it. She could hear labored breathing and footfalls kicking up stone and soil. And then she saw it—the obscure shadow of a man exiting the schoolyard, running obliquely across the street, coming toward them. It was the same man she had seen earlier. She couldn't be wrong. She had to rely on her senses. She had to trust her ears. She had to believe her eyes.

You must see it too, Julia. Why aren't you telling me to run? Why aren't you running? Why aren't you shouting—screaming?

"Run, Julia! Run!" Mary shouted. She pulled her dress up above her ankle and fled as fast as she could down Hobson Street. Behind her, she could hear Julia following close. She must have heard it too, because she was running now, running as fast and as hard as she was. When she made the left onto Dorset Street, her legs were aching and her chest was pounding, but panic pushed her on, closer to her room where she knew she would be safe.

Run faster, Julia, he's getting closer. He's right behind you now!

At last, she saw the narrow archway leading to Miller's Court. She was thankful her door was the one nearest the archway. But when she reached into her apron pocket for her key—it was not there!

Where had she put the key?

Julia came up behind her, breathing hard. "Hurry," she said.

Mary reached into a second apron pocket, but it was empty. Frantically, she plunged her hand into her coat pocket, and after rummaging through some old buttons, a box of matches and a few hairpins; she found the key beneath a crumpled hanky. With an unsteady hand, she probed the darkness for the keyhole, her knees weakening under the weight of growing terror. She had to unlock the door before she fell to the pavement in a swirling vortex of unconsciousness.

Behind her, the sound of running boots was suddenly louder and closer. It was too late for her to unlock the door, too late for her to get to safety. The murdering Devil was behind her now. She could feel his foul breath on her neck, his rough sweaty hands around her throat squeezing the life from her, and the cold steel of his knife blade as it sliced through the soft flesh of her throat, adding yet, another victim to his cavalcade of butchery.

"Quick!" Julia shouted. "Quick with the door!" She snatched the key from Mary's hand and forced it into the keyhole. With a hard turn and a push, the door opened. Shoving Mary in before her, Julia rushed into the room and quickly closed and locked the door behind them. She dropped the key into her pocket and then leaned against the doorframe to catch her breath. Mary stood motionless in the silent darkness, waiting, fearing, listening to Julia's rapid breathing, and her own, just as rapid and filled with terror. After a short while, she dared to whisper, "Is he gone?"

Julia walked to the small window and pulled back the soiled cloth Mary had been using
for a curtain. The night was still and quiet. "I don't see or hear a thing," she said.

"I heard the running and saw the figure of a man more than once," Mary said. "You heard it yourself."

Julia offered no confirmation as she carefully replaced the cloth over the window again, blocking out the night.

How could Julia not have heard or seen what I had? Mary thought. *The sound was real. The figure was there.*

"Well, we're safe now," Julia said.

"I'm sure," Mary said, although she wasn't sure. "I'll make a fire. The warmth will make us both feel better."

Instinctively she made her way to a nightstand, found several loose matches in the top drawer and lit a small lamp. The dim light revealed a narrow room with a single bed, two wooden chairs, a corner cupboard and a small fireplace against the far wall. After wiping the perspiration from her face with the bottom of her apron, she removed her coat and shawl and tossed them onto the bed. She got on her knees before the hearth and placed several pieces of kindling and a sheet from yesterday's post on the grate. Her hands were still trembling as she struck a match and touched it to the paper.

"I've never been so afraid in my life," she said. "They need to find this bloke before he has us all in the graveyard."

There was silence in the room behind her until Julia said, "They'll never find him."

"How can you be sure?" Mary said.

"Because they've got their noses in the wrong places," Julia said. And then there was an ominous shrill laugh that resounded in the darkness behind Mary. She turned and looked up at Julia, who was still standing by the window. In the flickering light of the new fire, something flashed for an instant, something bright and shining. It was the knife Julia had removed from her coat pocket as she raised it above her head and moved menacingly toward Mary.

The Thing in The Closet

"Did you hear something in the closet?" Harold said.

"I didn't hear anything," Wally answered, his eyes, ears, and mind engrossed on his video game console as he lounged on Harold's bed on the other side of the room.

"I know I heard a sound," Harold said. "I think it's come back."

Wally looked up at Harold with sudden interest. "You think who came back?" he said.

"Not *who*," Harold said, "but *what*?"

Annoyed at having been disturbed, but curious, Wally shut down his game console and looked over at the closet. It was a big closet, a walk-in, with one big door with open slots at the bottom. It would be easy to hear any sounds coming from inside. But how could anyone or anything have gotten into the closet? He and Harold had been studying most of the day in Harold's room and no one has come in or gone out of the house since his mother left for shopping.

"There it is again, Harold said. "Something's moving around in there."

"Something?" Wally said. He got off the bed and started toward the closet.

"Don't go near it!" Harold shouted. "There's something evil in there."

Wally stopped after taking a few steps, surprised and concerned. "Whoa, man," he said. "You've been reading too much Poe."

Night Dreams and Night Screams | 111

The Thing in The Closet

"I mean it," Harold said. He got up from his desk, grabbed Wally's arm, and pulled him away from the closet. "Don't go in there. Sit back down. I'll explain everything."

Wally sat on the edge of Harold's bed and waited for a plausible explanation. Harold went back to his desk and sat, then closed his computer screen before he began. "I know this sounds crazy," he said, "but I've been hearing sounds from inside my closet for the past week."

"What kind of sounds?' Wally said.

"Nothing I can explain," Harold said. "Just sounds, movement, like something's in there."

"Doing what?"

"I don't know."

"How often have you heard these sounds?"

"Mostly at night—late. But today is the first time I've heard them in the daytime."

"Have you seen anyone—or thing?"

"No. I just hear it moving around and sometimes I see moving shadows."

"Has anyone else seen or heard this thing?"

"It's only in my closet," Harold said.

"What would something be doing in your closet? Wally said. "And how would it get in there?"

"I don't know," Harold said. "You're asking me questions I don't have answers to. I only know something's in there and it's in there for no good reason. I believe when it's ready, it'll come out to cause terrible harm."

Wally could see Harold was genuinely afraid of whatever he believed was living in his closet. He could see the fear in his eyes and the sweat breaking out on his forehead as he spoke about it.

"You'd better take a deep breath," he said. "What you're telling me makes no sense."

Harold jumped up suddenly and cast a fearful look at the closet door. "There it is again," he said. "See how the door moved." He pointed a shaky finger at the door for Wally to see, but when Wally looked, he neither saw nor heard anything unusual. "I think you've been studying too hard or drinking too much beer," he said. He walked closer to Harold, placed his arms on his shoulders and gently guided him back into his chair. He could feel Harold trembling.

"Don't make jokes," Harold said. He stood up again, pushed passed Wally and walked across the room to his bed, keeping a wary eye on the closet door. Kneeling beside the bed, he reached beneath it and brought out a worn shoebox. He carried it back to his desk and laid it down carefully. When he opened the lid, Wally saw the box contained a nickel-plated 9mm handgun.

"Where'd you get that?"

"It belonged to my Dad," Harold said. "He kept it in the house for protection. I keep it under my bed now."

"What're you going to do with it?"

"Whatever I have to," Harold said. He took the gun out of the box and the fully loaded magazine beside it and slid the magazine into the gun with a loud *click*.

"I want to be ready when that thing comes out of the closet," Harold said.

"You better be careful with that," Wally said. "Somebody could get hurt."

"I know how to handle a gun," Harold said, releasing the safety and laying the gun down carefully on the desk with its muzzle pointed toward the closet.

Wally was beginning to feel uncomfortable with Harold's behavior. Although Harold had been under a ton of stress since his father unexpectedly left his mother, nearly a month ago—putting the obligation of "man of the house" solely on Harold's shoulders—he had never seen his friend act this way. No one knew for sure why Harold's father suddenly disappeared, marital problems were the consensus in the neighborhood.

Harold's relationship with his father had been tenuous at best. He had confided in Wally that he held ill feelings toward

The Thing in The Closet

his father and believed his father was physically abusing his mother. After Wally swore an oath of secrecy, Harold recalled to him how he had laid in his bed at night listening to the sounds his mother made, muffled cries of pain and abuse emanating through the wall between their bedroom and his. He had even heard the sounds his father made, and the sounds they made together. He had fallen asleep many nights with his pillow pressed against his ears, tears in his eyes as hatred for his father grew in his heart.

Harold carried his burden of anger and frustration for a long time, helpless to do anything until it began to affect him emotionally. His mother, finally realizing her son's sudden inordinate behavior, set up the sessions with Doctor Nugent. The Doctor had assured Harold's mother that together they would resolve just what was troubling Harold, but that it would take time and patience and understanding. Wally had been doing his part to bring things back to normal for his best friend, but this afternoon had been a setback, Harold was seeing and hearing things that weren't there. He'd have to mention it to Harold's mom so she could bring it to the attention of Doctor Nugent before things got worse.

"Have you looked in the closet?" Wally said.

"No way."

"Then how can you be sure something's in there?"

"I told you, I see shadows moving and hear weird sounds."

"Is it always in there?"

"I hear it mostly at night. It comes and goes."

"What do you think it wants?"

"I don't know, but it's not here for a friendly visit."

Wally stepped closer to the closet door.

"Don't go near it!" Harold shouted.

"I want to look inside," Wally said.

"No. You'll let it out. It'll kill us all."

"If it wants to come out," Wally said. "There's nothing to stop it."

The Thing in The Closet

"It'll come out when the time is right," Harold said.

Harold was working himself into a frenzy and Wally was beginning to fear for his own safety. He thought it best to try and get the gun away from Harold and put it back under the bed out of Harold's sight—and mind. He wished Harold's mother would get back from shopping soon.

"Give me the gun," Wally said. He reached for the gun on the desk, but Harold snatched it up and held it close by his side. "No. The gun stays with me," he said.

"But I want to take it with me and see who is in there."

"I told you, you can't go in there. You'll cause us all to die."

Wally walked closer to Harold and put on his serious face. "Listen to me, if there is something in that closet and it's as terrible as you think it is, then we'd better find out just what it is, and stop it from doing whatever awful thing it's here to do."

Harold contemplated this reasoning and then said, "But if we disturb it, or upset it, we might be putting ourselves in worse jeopardy. At least now it's content to stay in the closet. I think we should leave it alone."

"Okay," Wally said, throwing up his hands. "If you wanna wait around until some night when that thing decides to come out and strangle you in your bed." Wally saw the terror grow on Harold's face. He put a consoling hand on his friend's shoulder. "Listen, buddy. Maybe there's nothing in the closet. Maybe you're just imagining it."

"I'm not," Harold said. "I've seen it moving around in there. I can hear it breathing in the darkness at night when I'm lying in bed."

"Then if there's something in there, let's find out what it is. Maybe it's a stray cat or a raccoon that got into the house and became trapped."

"It's a lot bigger than a cat," Harold said. "I've seen its shadow as it passes the door. It has massive shoulders and a huge head and it stands almost as high as the ceiling. And it gives off a foul stench. Can't you smell it?"

The Thing in The Closet

Wally offered no confirmation but walked back toward Harold's bed, closer to the closet. "I'm going inside," he said. "If there's something in there, I'm gonna find it."

"Don't do it, Wally," Harold yelled, as he stood ridged, almost petrified with fear at the thought of Wally confronting the thing in the closet. His body began to tremble as he gripped the gun tighter in his hand and watched Wally approach the closet door. Wally stopped for a moment and leaned his ear against the door. Cautiously, he put his hand on the door handle and pulled the door open.

"Don't," Harold begged. "Don't go in." Ignoring Harold's warning, Wally took a careful step into the semi-darkness and let the door close behind him.

There was silence in the room as Harold waited a long agonizing time.

I *need to protect Wally*, he thought. *He doesn't realize what he's doing. I can't let that thing get to him.*

Slowly, mechanically, he raised the gun in both his hands and pointed it at the closet door, waiting for the inevitable screams and cries to come from Wally as the thing in the closet—provoked and angry—unleashed its rage upon his friend.

Harold stood in the silence, his body nearly convulsing in anticipation and fear until he saw the yellow light around the edges of the doorframe when Wally flicked on the interior light switch. "There's no one in here, Harold," Wally finally said, his voice echoing inside the hollow closet. "Just a bunch of empty clothes hangers and an old trunk in the corner."

"Don't open it," Harold said. "The thing might be in there."

"I have to see what's in it," Wally said.

"No, don't open it!' Harold screamed, even as he heard Wally releasing the trunks metal latch.

"Don't open the trunk," he shouted again. But the squealing of the hinges told him it was too late. Wally had lifted the lid.

There was an ominous silence from within the closet until Wally finally said, "You're right, Harold, there *is* something in it."

The Thing in The Closet

"Leave it alone," Harold pleaded.

The gun was shaking in his hands now, pointed straight at the closet door.

"It looks like …it looks like a body," Wally said. "A dead body!"

"Don't! Don't!" Harold shouted.

"It *is* a body, Wally said. " Oh, my God. It's…it's your—"

A single shot rang out, sending a bullet through the closet door, and through Wally's spine. Without a sound, Wally dropped to the closet floor—dead.

***

The car door slammed and jolted him upright. He had fallen asleep at his desk with his head on his arms, the gun still in his hand. His mother had returned home from shopping.

He looked around his room, everything seemed as it should be. He didn't know how long he had been asleep nor where Wally had gone. He put the gun away in the top drawer of his desk and waited calmly as he listened to his mother close the front door to the house and walk into the kitchen. His head felt heavy and his temples ached. He rubbed the sleep from his eyes and brushed back his hair to compose himself, knowing his mother would come up to his room when she was ready. If something looked untoward she would start with the questions, just like Doctor Nugent. Questions—questions— and more questions, he was sick of questions, if they would just leave him alone long enough to—

"Harold, I'm home," his mother shouted up to him. She was already on her way up to his room; he could hear her footsteps on the stairs. He opened his laptop and the screen flickered to life just as his mother appeared in his doorway.

"Am I interrupting?" she said.

She stepped into the room offering him her phony smile. It was the smile he had come to hate. The smile she had hid behind all the while *he* was doing those things to her. The same smile she

The Thing in The Closet

had used to deny the abuse and punishment he had been putting her through, protecting that sick bastard for whatever reason she had. He had always loved his mother but lately, she seemed as phony and untrusting as his father had been. Maybe she didn't mind what he had been doing to her. Maybe she enjoyed it.

She walked over and kissed his forehead. "Have you been studying all afternoon?" she said.

"Wally and I have been working on that school project."

He tried to remember why Wally had to leave so suddenly, but couldn't. He would ask Wally about it in the morning.

He watched her walk to his bed and sit.

She likes the bed, he thought. *Their bed is where he did things to her; where she allowed him to do those things.*

He watched her as she looked around the room, visually examining everything that belonged to him: his bed, his dresser, his bookshelf, his desk...his closet. She was looking for something out of the ordinary, something she could find fault with so she could correct him or reprimand him like she'd always done. She was forever treating him like a child. He wasn't a child and he was beginning to hate her for it.

"When are you going to tidy up your room?" she said.

Questions!

"I haven't had time," he said.

"I've asked you twice this week already."

"I'll get to it,"

"You told me that days ago," she said. "If you're not going to help me keep—"

He stood up from his chair suddenly and placed his finger over his lips, indicating for her to stop talking. In the quietness of the room, she watched curiously as he fixed his eyes on the closet door. He stood motionless for nearly a full minute until she finally said, "What is it, Harold?"

"Did you hear something in the closet?" he said.

The Devil's Details

Be sober, be vigilant; because your adversary the devil, as a roaring lion, walks about seeking whom he may devour.
                                                    Peter 5:8

"I need a soul," the Devil said, "and one of you will give me yours."

Burt Wilson stood up from his seat by the campfire and said, "I don't think so."

The Devil licked his lips delicately with his pointed tongue and smiled.

"I think you will," he said.

Burt and his buddies had been sitting around the fire after a good day of hunting. They had put down a hearty supper and were drinking beer and telling small lies about themselves when the Devil walked out of the forest and into their firelight. He was thin but muscular and dressed entirely in black from his polished boots to a satin long sleeve shirt, buttoned at the wrists and collar but with no tie. His black hair was slicked back tight against his head as was the skin of his face, which accented his high cheekbones and beak-like nose. His skin appeared a deep crimson—or was that just the light from the campfire? When he spoke, a full set of pointed white teeth contrasted with his black lips and dark, deep-set eyes. The Devil leaned against a tree and folded his arms comfortably over his chest. "As a rule, I am not a fair player," he began, "but in this case, I'll allow you to choose which one among you will come with me. There are details, however, that must be—"

"Nobody can make me give up my soul," Burt interrupted.

The Devil scowled at Burt. The flames from the campfire danced on the Devil's face as he paused, then, continued. "Details that must be clearly understood," he said. "Contrary to popular belief, I cannot *take* a righteous soul. It must be *given* to me willingly, offered in exchange for something."

"If you can't take a soul," Doc said, "then you have no power over us."

"But I do," the Devil said. "My usual threats, offerings, manipulations and bribes, and a plethora of sordid deals. My bag of tricks is full and has served me well for centuries."

"Why one of us?" Carl Foley said.

"As it happens, you are all suitable candidates. Each of you is confronted with a dilemma in your life, a problem you wish would go away, a viable bargaining chip if you will."

He removed a slender cigar from his breast pocket and held it in his lips while he touched it to a blue flame that appeared between his fingertips. He took a long drag and let the smoke out slowly before he continued.

"Frankly, I can't see why anyone would be willing to trade his or her soul, it is such a precious commodity. Even though it has negligible value here on earth, it can become quite useful when the time comes. Nevertheless, you'd be surprised what people will ask in exchange for it."

Burt stepped out in front of the others and moved closer to the Devil. He was big and brawny and had spent long years working at the lumber mill before he retired last summer. Now he wanted to get a better look at this intruder. "Who are you, mister?" Burt demanded.

"I'm whoever you want me to be," the Devil answered.

The Devil's Details

Allan Wanamaker rolled his wheelchair away from the fire, closer to Burt. He adjusted his glasses to get a better look at this stranger and said, "Are you claiming to be the Devil?"

"You know as much about me as I know about you," the Devil answered.

"What do you know about me?" Allan said.

The Devil took another long drag from his cigar and said, "I know you were in an automobile accident seven years ago, your wife and daughter were killed and you've been in that wheelchair ever since. A bit too much to drink that night, Allan?"

Allan hung his head under the weight of guilt.

"I also know you'll never walk again."

"That's not true, Allan said. "The doctors said—"

"I know what I know," the Devil interrupted.

Carl jumped up from his seat. "This guy's a nutcase!" he said. "Why we listening to him?"

"Where'd you come from, mister?" Burt said. "And how'd you get here?"

"It doesn't matter. I'm here on business, so let's get at it."

While they watched with cautious curiosity, the Devil dropped his cigar onto the pine needle floor and crushed it out under his boot. He moved to a large tree stump nearby and sat on it. Scanning the faces before him, he pointed a long finger at Doc.

"Doctor Judson Purcell, fifty-six, Harvard Medical School, Phi Beta Kappa, married eighteen years, two sons and a daughter. Enjoys a lucrative practice and an affluent lifestyle, a squeaky clean pillar of the community—that is, until Margaret McCauley jingled your bells."

Doc scowled, as the others looked at him surprised by this revelation.

"I'm sure if Mrs. Purcell were to find out about this impropriety, your perfect life would crumble rather quickly."

"You're crazy," Doc said. "Don't believe his lies."

"Don't worry," the Devil said. "The sordid facts disclosed here today will be forgotten by all of you as soon as you leave here."

"Your threats won't work with us," Burt said.

"They always have," the Devil assured him.

"What've you got to say about me?" Carl challenged. He stood up, put his hands on his ample hips and waited for an answer.

The Devil gently stroked the hairs on his chin before speaking. Carl couldn't help noticing this stranger's slender fingers were tipped with small black talons. When he was ready, the Devil said, "Carlton Foley, aged, fifty-one, married, no children, senior partner in the accounting firm of Foley & Ruskin and currently under investigation for allegedly embezzling from his own company. If you're convicted, you can spend the rest of your life in prison."

"That's a damned lie!" Carl shouted.

"Not this time," the Devil said. "But I can fabricate a convincing lie when I need to. It's one of my stronger talents."

Burt had been keeping his eye on the hunting guns where they had left them leaning against the outside wall of the camper. If he could get to one, he might be able to scare off this wacko. He took several aggressive steps closer to the Devil but stopped when a shimmering aura suddenly encircled the tree stump and began to pulsate, threateningly. Burt stepped back wisely and waited as the aura faded.

"You cannot threaten me with physical harm," the Devil said. "It's been tried by the best and cannot be accomplished by mortal beings. Let's proceed."

He pointed his finger at Burt. "Burton Wilson," he said, "forty-four, laborer, lumberjack, great white hunter and purveyor of this expedition. Divorced five years and living the bachelor's life, but that little cutie you picked up at Brennan's bar and had your way with is about to yell rape to the police. Did you check her ID, Burt? She was little more than a child."

"She said she was— I mean, I never— "

"You should have checked, Burt," the Devil chided. "The bitch could ruin your whole life." And he let out a loud laugh that reverberated through the trees and echoed in the dark forest, stirring up a wind that carried twigs and leaves in a whirlpool around the camp. The laugh was so thunderous it hurt their ears and they covered them with their hands until the laughter and wind subsided.

During this distraction, Burt had been inching his way closer to the camper. He was close enough now to snatch up a shotgun. The Devil was still laughing when Burt saw his chance, grabbed a gun, swung it in the direction of the stump and fired. The gunshot fractured the darkness causing the others to drop to the ground in surprise. When the smoke dissipated and they could see the stump, the Devil had vanished.

"Are you crazy?" Carl shouted, getting back to his feet. "You want to piss him off? You heard what he said about physical harm."

Burt ran to the stump and looked behind it. "He's not here," he said. "I scared him off."

"You can't scare the Devil," Doc said.

"Well he's gone," Burt said.

Allan was looking upward from his wheelchair at something across the campsite "I don't think he is," he said.

The others followed Allan's gaze up to the reaching limbs of a nearby tree. The full moon hung in the cloudless sky like a new silver dollar and the silhouette of the Devil sitting comfortably on a tree limb was visible within it.

"You need to hone your hunting skills," the Devil said.

They watched in amazement as he floated down from the limb and landed in front of them. He scowled at Burt, and when he wiggled his finger at the shotgun Burt was holding, the gun turned to dust and fell to Burt's feet.

"Now that you've gotten that out of your system," he said, "I'll continue with the details." Resignedly, Burt walked back to the others while the Devil returned to his seat on the stump.

"Each of you currently faces a grave dilemma in your life, a tradable commodity, shall we say. I've made it easier for you to offer a trade by bringing them to light. My part of the bargain is to make your problem disappear or to grant some other desire you may have. Collectively, you must decide which one of you will come with me tonight."

"Let me understand this," Doc said. "If we give up one of our souls, you will then eradicate the other problems, make them go away, and let the others go."

"Yes," the Devil said. "Three for one, not a bad deal coming from me."

"What if none of us chooses to go with you?"

"Then we could be here until one of you does. Time is of no concern to me."

"You'll hold us against our will?"

"Let's say we are negotiating a contract which may or may not take us a long while. The choice is entirely yours."

"I thought a person's soul was collected after they die," Doc said.

"It can be if it's part of an agreement. In this case, I need to expedite things."

"But that means one of us would have to—"

"I favor the term, 'move on'," the Devil said.

"But the one who loses his soul gets nothing in the bargain," Doc said.

"These are my terms," was the reply.

The Devil got up and walked away from them.

"I'll leave you to make your decision," he said, without looking back. "You must make a choice, tonight." And with that, he vanished into the trees.

They all stood in perplexed silence, unsure of what to do next until Carl spoke.

"We're in a tough spot. He's forcing us to bargain with him."

"Let's sit down and think about this," Doc said. "As unbelievable as all this is, there must be a way out."

They returned to their chairs around the campfire and sat quietly amongst the nocturnal sounds of the forest, each one waiting for someone else to speak first.

"Let's just get out of here," Burt finally said. "Leave everything, pile into the camper and go."

"That's dumb," Carl said. "He's probably watching us right now."

"Well he's got us where he wants us," Doc said. "Seems to me we have no alternative but to make a decision."

"Decide which one of us is gonna trade their soul to him?" Burt said.

"How can we decide that?" Carl said.

"Anyone have a better idea?"

"Maybe we can make a deal so he'll let us all go," Burt suggested.

"He wants a soul," Carl said. "That's the only deal he'll make. If we don't give him one, there's no telling what he'll do."

"Well, how can we choose whose soul he'll get?" Burt said.

"A volunteer would make things easier," Doc said.

"Would that be you?" Carl said.

"Oh no," Doc said. "I can dump Margaret McCauley tomorrow. You're facing a jail sentence; at your age, they'll probably carry you out of prison. You've got more reason to trade than me."

"I'll take my chance with the law," Carl said.

"I say we jump him," Burt said.

"A rape conviction could put you away for a long time," Carl said. "Maybe you'd better start thinking about making a trade and stop talking stupid."

Burt reached out and grabbed Carl by his shirtfront. "Who you callin' stupid?" he said. "And I didn't rape nobody. I don't care what that guy says."

"Take it easy," Doc said. "Let's not lose our civility over this. Let's settle down and start thinking logically."

"There's nothing logical about this," Allan said. "It's like a nightmare."

"Well we better think of something or he'll never set us free," Carl reminded.

"Since he can't take a soul, he's forcing us to give him one," Doc said. "He's a master of manipulation. We'd better be cautious."

"How about if the oldest of us gives up his soul," Burt suggested.

"That'd be you, Doc," Allan noted.

"At least it's a criteria, but I'm not feeling very charitable right now."

"It's our fault that we're in this predicament," Allan said. "We've made ourselves the object of his quarry by the sins we carry."

"All except you," Doc said. "He never mentioned a sin of yours, Allan. Don't you have one?"

"We're all sinners to some degree," Allan said.

"Would you trade your soul to be able to walk again?" Burt said.

"Of course he wouldn't," Carl said. "He's better off here in that wheelchair than having two good legs in Hell."

"Which one of us has the least to lose," Doc said.

"Allan," Burt said. "He lost his family and he's stuck in that wheelchair forever. What does he have to look forward to?"

"Who appointed you God?" Allan shouted. "Why don't you give up your worthless soul?"

"Now, hold on," Doc said. "Nobody's playing God."

Allan threw a contemptuous look at Burt, "I need a drink," he said. He pushed his wheelchair up the makeshift ramp they had built for him and disappeared into the camper.

"Why'd you say that?" Doc said to Burt.

"It's the truth," Burt said.

"Maybe, but you shouldn't have said it."

"Well I'm not giving up my soul," Burt said.

"Me neither," Carl said.

"Whether we like it or not, we have to make a decision or we'll never get out of these woods."

"Doc's right," Carl said. "We're just putting off the inevitable."

The Devil's Details

Allan appeared at the camper door and maneuvered his wheelchair down the ramp to rejoin the others.

"Why don't we take a vote," Carl suggested. "A secret ballot."

"It's a fair idea," Doc said. "No one will know how the other guy voted. Each of us will write the name of the person he thinks should surrender his soul to save the rest of us. The name with the most votes will give up his soul."

"I can't think of a better way out of this," Carl said.

"It's scary, Burt said, "but I'll go along with it."

"I won't vote," Allan said. "It's a stupid idea."

"You got a better one?" Burt said.

"We could try prayer," Allan said.

"Prayer?" Burt shouted. "You think we can beat the Devil with prayer?"

"It's been done before," Allan said.

"We don't have time for prayer," Doc said. "We'll take a vote."

"I won't be a part of it," Allan said.

"Then we'll vote without you," Doc said, "but you'll abide by the outcome."

He went into the camper and brought back a pencil and several sheets of notepaper and handed a sheet to Carl and one to Burt. After they had made their choice, they dropped their ballot into the bottom of Doc's hat. Before he started the count, Doc said. "We're all being punished here. Whatever the outcome, we'll have to live with it for the rest of our lives."

They knew Doc was right as they sat by the campfire in thoughtful silence and watched him read the votes, hoping someone would come up with a better solution. No one did.

***

"A satisfactory conclusion!"

The voice bellowed out of the darkness. They looked in the direction of the tree stump to see the Devil standing in front of it, his legs apart, his hands placed assertively on his hips and his eyes glowing red with excited anticipation.

Burt stood up and approached him with clenched fists. An aura surrounded the Devil quickly, but this time Burt stood his ground.

"If there was some way I could beat you, I would," he said.

The Devil laughed. "Indeed, mortals have tried," he said.

Allan waited for the aura to subside, then pushed his wheelchair closer to the Devil, and for the first time, he could smell the stench of evil the Devil carries with him.

"If you take one of us tonight," he said, "the others will be set free?"

"Correct," the Devil said.

"How can we trust you?" Burt said.

"You can't," the Devil answered.

Doc and Carl got up from their seats and walked closer to the others.

"We've taken a vote," Doc said.

"An admirable attempt at fairness," the Devil said. "And you've made the right choice, as I hoped you would."

"I thought our choice didn't matter to you," Carl said.

"Your individual choice doesn't," the Devil said, "but collectively I've proven, once again, the egoism of human beings."

"What are you getting at?" Doc said.

"You've all chosen to give me a soul, but your choice is less important to me than your motive."

"Why should you care?" Burt said. "A soul is a soul."

"Not so," the Devil said. "The ideal soul for me is one of evil, bloated with sin and doomed to perdition. These souls are mine for the taking. I have no power over righteous souls. There is a place for those, but not with me. The three of you have chosen this invalid to relinquish his soul to me, thus, procuring freedom for yourselves. But you have failed."

"How have we failed?" Doc said.

The Devil's Details

"You should have been more diligent in your struggle to keep your souls," the Devil added. "A collaborative effort might have made you victorious, but instead, you took the easy way out and your decision has demonstrated to me that you possess iniquitous souls, unfeeling and self-serving. Consequently, you have enabled me to take the three of you with me, tonight."

"You're taking *all* our souls?" Burt said.

"A bounty larger than I had expected," the Devil said with a broad smile.

"And what happens to Allan?"

"He keeps his soul," the Devil said, "it has no place with me."

"But you said you couldn't take a soul," Burt reminded.

"I cannot take a *righteous* soul," the Devil corrected.

"This is crazy," Carl said. "It wasn't supposed to be this way."

"I'm afraid we've been duped," Doc conceded.

The Devil threw his head back and laughed.

"It's all in the details," he said.

The Visitation

There were five murders committed inside McGovern's mansion—actually, four murders and a suicide. The mansion stood on the hill overlooking the town of Sheepstead for more than ninety years, and if the town fathers hadn't made it a candidate for the wrecking ball, it would have probably stood for another ninety. There was nothing magnificent about the place, except it was big and ornate with spires and cupolas. An ivy-covered stone wall surrounded the property and there was a wrought-iron gate at the entrance where a brick walkway made its way up to the front portico.

Since Jonas McGovern built the mansion in the last century as a wedding gift for his new bride, it had been surrounded by unwarranted mystery and rumor, although nothing extraordinary had ever been documented about the place, until the murders last year. Two generations of McGovern's had lived and died there, and after the murders, the house was left to the residents of Sheepstead. The locals had no idea what to do with it, so it stood neglected for a long while. Of course, a structure of such longevity simply had to inhabit ghosts; most of the residents of Sheepstead believed so—especially after the murders.

When I was shining shoes down at the barbershop, I listened to the older men tell ghost stories about the place. Each swore his story was true, and some I'd heard caused the hairs on my forearms to stand on end. My father said there were no such things as ghosts and the men at the barbershop had nothing better to do than tells tales. He said he had heard the same stories when he was my age. I thought about that and figured, if these stories had been passed down through two generations, there just might be some truth in them. Besides, at sixteen, I wasn't so sure there wasn't such a thing as a ghost.

Since my mother's unexpected death last year, my father hadn't been himself; and although her passing was just as difficult for me, I felt an inherent obligation to keep him as content and normal as possible under the circumstance. He took her passing hard and although he confessed to me that he felt responsible for her death; he was in no way to blame.

After the paper mill closed, my father spent months looking for work, but to no avail. What little money my parents had saved soon became exhausted. The mortgage payments had gotten behind and the utilities nearly cut off more than once. The money I earned shining shoes did little to alleviate our financial crisis. When my father suggested my mother find employment to help with the finances, she was more than willing to go to work.

"The McGovern's need a cook," she'd said, seated at the kitchen table over the morning paper. My father sipped his coffee and said nothing. Although it had been his idea, he wasn't comfortable with the thought of my mother going to work. In all their married years, he had been the breadwinner and my mother the homemaker. That's the way he liked it and that's the way it should be, he'd said. I realized years later just how much he loved and worshipped my mother and to ask her to support him now, seemed to him, to negate everything he had ever done for her.

The police said Wade McGovern just snapped. No one knew exactly why. Some guessed he was terminally ill and chose to take his own life rather than go out the hard way, others claimed he'd been caught in a financial scandal and feared the impending consequences. Although theories abound, no one knew for sure—including the police—why Wade McGovern went off the deep end that Sunday afternoon in August.

The Visitation

But most of all, no one could understand why he'd decided to take everyone else in the house with him: his wife of twenty years, their sixteen-year-old daughter and fourteen-year-old son, and…my mother.

It happened while my mother was preparing the family's evening meal. Wade took his handgun from the drawer next to his bed, loaded it with 9mm rounds and methodically eliminated himself and everyone around him that quiet Sunday afternoon. He shot his wife from an upstairs window while she was on her knees weeding her garden and dispatched his daughter while she studied her homework at her desk in her bedroom. His namesake son was shot from behind while he worked on the engine of his car in the garage. My mother was at the stove in the kitchen when he came upon her. Afterward, he sat in his favorite chair in the library, wrapped his lips tightly around the muzzle of his gun and pulled the trigger. No suicide note was found and his motive is still unknown.

No one was aware the crimes had been committed until my mother was late coming home, and my father, concerned about her lateness, phoned the mansion. When he repeatedly received no answer, he notified the police. The carnage was discovered that evening.

"What happened to mom wasn't your fault," I said to him one evening at the dinner table when I knew he was feeling exceptionally low. The unwarranted burden of guilt he'd placed on himself turned his sandy hair a light gray and the haggardness in his face made him appear older than his years.

"If I hadn't pushed her to get a job—" he said, staring down at his dinner plate wearing that mask of remorse that had become so familiar to me.

"But you didn't," I said. "Mom was eager to help."

"She was always willing to sacrifice for us," he said. "That's why I love her so."

"Me too," I said.

He looked up at me with an approving smile.

The Visitation

"Even though she's no longer with us, I know she's happy," I said.

He lost his smile and looked at me hard.

"How could you know that?" he asked.

I hesitated before I answered. "Sometimes at night, she speaks to me."

My father became suddenly agitated. "Your mother is dead," he said. "The dead don't talk to the living."

"She wants you to know the truth," I said daringly. "She told me to—"

"There are no such things as ghosts!" he interrupted. "What's gone is gone forever! You've been listening to too many fool stories. I won't have you desecrate your mother's memory by claiming to have talked to ghosts."

The weight of my words weren't enough to change my father's mind. He carried the guilt of her death with him no matter how much I tried to make him see the truth. I only hoped he wouldn't succumb to his self-imposed condemnation to the point where I'd lose him too.

There were several moments of silence between us before I said, "I love mom too, and miss her a lot."

He looked at me through moist eyes, forcing a smile back to his face. "We'll always have that," he said. *"When you truly love someone that love never dies—not ever."*

I smiled back at him, and we finished our dinner without another word about it.

The following day, I took my usual route home from school, passing the mansion as I regularly did. Although it had been shrouded in mystery for years, I had never feared the place, but instead, had acquired a strange connection to it after my mother had taken employment there. I followed the sidewalk along the stonewall until I came to the iron gate, which stood before the brick walkway that led to the front entrance. I paused to look up at that edifice of horror, scanning the darkened windows that looked out at the world like portentous eyes, and at the

The Visitation

spires as they pierced the approaching storm clouds passing low over the roofline.

As my eyes focused on the front door, I felt as though something was drawing me closer to the house. I had never visited the mansion while my mother worked there, but now, I was compelled to go inside and found myself following the walkway toward the front entrance almost against my will.

I walked between the pillars of the front portico, overgrown now with clinging vines and tall grass, and stopped in front of the massive front door. Fearlessly, I pushed the door back and stepped into the darkened main hallway. The repugnant odor of age and neglect hit me like a fist. Only the daylight filtering through the windows guided me as I moved deeper into the mansion, and it took several minutes for my eyes to adjust to the semi-darkness.

I made my way down the long hallway, passing empty rooms where people had spent their lives, rooms forever silent with well-kept secrets that had been held for nearly a century. As I walked, an irrepressible feeling that I was not alone came over me. And although the eeriness of the place would set anyone's heart-pounding—strangely, I wasn't afraid. I passed cobweb enshrouded sconce lamps and framed oil painting of long-gone McGovern ancestry mounted on walls of flowered wallpaper.

When I came to the entrance of a large sitting room, curiosity pushed me through the double doors. The ambiance and furnishings instantly transported me back to an earlier time. There was a large sofa and several armchairs in the center of the room, and in a far corner, a grand piano stood, silent and forgotten. Rows of dust-laden books on shelves that reached almost to the vaulted ceiling stood against one wall and through the floor to ceiling windows I could see the skeletal limbs of the Sycamore trees swaying in the wind, scratching at the glass-like searching human arms.

Although the approaching storm had darkened the room, the occasional flash of lightning lit everything like daylight while the surroundings shuddered with each crescendo of thunder that followed.

The Visitation

I backed into a dark corner, squeezed my eyes shut and covered my ears with my hands until the sounds of the storm subsided. When I opened my eyes, they were immediately drawn to movement across the room. Squinting through the darkness, I could see a translucent figure appearing in a distant doorway, barely perceptible at first, but then growing larger and more apparent. I was unable to believe what I was seeing, yet unwilling to turn my eyes away. At first, I thought the storm had been playing tricks on me, but as the figure emerged from the shadows; I was able to discern what appeared to be a boy about my age. He wandered into the room without emotion, stopped and turned his head slowly from side to side as if searching for something or someone. I squeezed my eyes shut again to dispel the illusion.

When I opened them, he was standing in the center of the room watching me. Through a shimmering haze, I could see denim overalls, work boots and a sleeveless shirt. His colorless face held no expression and contrasted with his dark hollow eyes. He held in his hand what appeared to be a rusted mechanic's wrench. I shivered when he fixed his sightless eyes on me in a cold stare, realizing I was the one he had been looking for. With unyielding curiosity, I watch him raise the wrench above his head, give out a piercing scream and hurl it in a wide arc in my direction. I dropped to the floor as the tool whizzed through the darkness, missing my head by inches and shattering the plaster in the wall behind me. With my heart pounding and my knees weak, I stayed low in the shadows as I watched him turn and walk silently back through the doorway from which he'd come. Only then was I able to see the gaping hole in the back of his head, and the resulting ugliness of a gunshot wound splattered across his neck and shoulders. I closed my eyes again to shut out the horror. When I opened them he was gone.

What had I seen? Was this the ghost of Wade McGovern's son, murdered by his father? Was this proof that the stories I'd heard at the barbershop were true?

The Visitation

Cautiously, I made my way back into the hallway as the storm outside intensified with howling wind and pelting rain. Despite what I had just witnessed, the growing fear inside me wasn't enough to make me run for the front door. Something was compelling me to stay. Something or someone was telling me there were answers here.

I continued along the dark hallway, hugging the cold walls, my eyes darting in every direction, wary but unwilling to turn back until I came to the doorway of a great dining room where I stopped to catch my breath. As I scanned the darkness of the room, I was suddenly jolted by a shrill scream as the specter of a young girl rushed through an open doorway across the room, waving her arms frantically in the air. Like the boy, she was devoid of color and I could see through her form as she ran passed—or should I say *through*—the dining table. Her scream bristled the hairs on the back of my neck as I saw a man appeared in the doorway behind her, brandishing a pistol.

He was as colorless and translucent as the girl as he ran into the room in pursuit of her. I hid behind the doorframe and watched as he paused, raised the pistol, took careful aim and fired. The gunshot reverberated over a clash of thunder as the muzzle blast turned the room orange-red. The girl's scream was cut short when the bullet struck her back, tearing a wide hole in her flesh and causing her to lurch forward before she fell to the floor.

The man stood over her, smiling like a proud hunter over his recently bagged game. His sardonic smile sent a chill through my body when he looked up at me, raised his pistol in my direction and fired. A bullet splintered the wooden doorframe close to my ear.

I turned and ran; sure my pursuer was close behind. I heard a second shot, and then another echo in the darkness behind me. I continued running until I found myself beneath the archway entrance of a large kitchen at the rear of the house. Leaning against the archway, I waited in the darkness, uncertain of what to do next.

The Visitation

What was I witnessing? Were these the spirits of Wade McGovern and his family, condemned to the mansion for eternity as some stories I'd heard had claimed? Was this evidence that ghosts do exist?

I was afraid and trembling and wanted to run, run as fast and as hard as I could toward the front door, but Wade McGovern was somewhere, waiting…waiting in the dark.

With a shaky hand, I removed my handkerchief from the back pocket of my jeans and wiped the perspiration from my face and forehead as I contemplated my next move. For the first time, I realized the rumblings of the storm had subsided and within the stillness, all I could hear was my heart pounding in my chest and my labored breathing. As I rested in the welcomed silence, I thought I heard from the depths of the darkness, what sounded like my father calling my name. When I listened harder, I heard his voice again and wondered if it was all just a piece of the illusion I had found myself a part of.

I strained my eyes to look down the hallway toward the front entrance and felt my body stiffen when I saw a vague figure moving quietly through the darkness toward me. I prepared myself for the worst; sure I was about to become Wade McGovern's next victim. I waited, helpless and afraid, as the figure moved silently toward me. And was surprised and relieved when I saw my father emerge from the shadows and into the dim window light. He was breathing hard, his face glistening with perspiration as he put his big hands on my shoulders. "When you didn't come home from school I began to worry," he said. "Why did you come here?"

"I don't know," I said. "How did you know where to find me?"

He was unable to give me an answer, until he finally said, "I'm not sure, something—"

"Told you to come," I said.

He gave me an incredulous look.

"What are you doing here?" he said.

"I've seen things, Dad," I said.

I could see frustration and doubt in his face when he asked, "What kind of things?"

How could I explain to a man as unbelieving as my father, the things that I had witnessed, things I could only interpret as a display of ghostly images? I stood there, trying to find the words, but they wouldn't come.

"You shouldn't have come here," he said.

"But there's a reason for my being here," I said. "And a reason why you're here now."

"There is no good reason," he said. "We're getting out of here."

He took my arm and began to lead me toward the front entrance, but stopped suddenly and looked curiously over my shoulder into the kitchen behind us. I turned and followed his gaze into the shadows but saw nothing. Before I could look back, he released my arm and walked through the kitchen archway. He stopped before a center table, his eyes affixed on something in the shadows beyond.

When I looked, I saw a misty image emerging from the murky darkness across the room. Just a floating mass of vapor as it moved closer to my father and began to take form. Had my friend with the mechanic's wrench returned or was this the ghost of Wade McGovern looking for another victim? I took a step closer to my father, prepared to defend him against this ghostly murderer, but stopped when the transformation of the figure became complete. A feeling of warm security came over me when I recognized my mother's tender smile.

She stopped at the table beside my father as her eyes met his. She looked as beautiful as I remembered her. Her auburn hair fell in soft folds over the milky whiteness of her shoulders and her eyes still sparkled with the warmth and understanding of the mother I knew. My father, overwhelmed by what he was seeing, gripped the edge of the table with his big hands to steady himself.

The Visitation

"Everything is all right, Richard," I heard my mother say in a soft voice. "Our time together has come and gone, but we'll always be together in spirit."

My father stood for a moment, unable to speak until he finally said, "But if I only hadn't insisted that you—"

"We did what we had to do," my mother said. "You mustn't blame yourself for what happened, but keep our love alive through our son. Go now and live the life we'd planned."

My father looked at me with paternal pride, then looked back at my mother.

"I'll always be with you," she said.

He reached for her hand, but she drew it back gracefully as she began to move away from him. "Keep our love, Richard," were her final words, as she dissolved back into the shadows. My father stood for a moment trying to digest all he had seen before walking back to me. He looked at me with a sense of satisfaction and relief. "She forgives me," he said.

"There was nothing to forgive," I said.

He put his arm over my shoulder as we walked down the long corridor and out the front door. The storm had passed, and the sky was bright as I walked beside him in thoughtful silence.

My father was right: *When you truly love someone, that love never dies—not ever.*

But he was wrong about ghosts.

The Secret of Skinny Bigelow

Alex McGrath confessed to me the secret he'd kept hidden inside himself for most of his adult life—the secret of Skinny Bigelow.

I had been McGrath's attorney for more than ten years and when his time came; he felt compelled to summon me to his deathbed to cleanse his soul. He needed to release himself, he said; free himself from the sin and its consequences that had been his punishment for so many years.

McGrath was eighty-six, and I was surprised he could recall the events with such detail. He looked at me through watery eyes, his voice weak, almost a whisper. Even with trembling lips, he was able to take me back to Hemlock Falls and the summer I turned sixteen.

McGrath was foreman up at the lumber mill in those days. He was big and brawny with forearms as thick as his thighs and shoulders as burly as the cut logs he'd carried on them, a stark contrast to the emaciated figure lying before me now. With lots of hard work and a little luck, in time, he became a partner in the mill, prospered and purchased the big house at the edge of town where he lived very comfortably with his wife and daughter.

As he spoke, he evoked my own memories of Skinny Bigelow. How incredibly thin Skinny was. There was nothing physically wrong with him; he was simply born that way. It was said of Skinny, if he turned sideways you couldn't hit him with a stone from ten feet. To add to his inordinate physique, he stood well over six feet and his long black hair, which hung straight to his shoulders, made him appear even taller. Some joked that if it weren't for Skinny's sizable nose, you wouldn't see him at all. Of course, these were gross exaggerations invented by the townsfolk of Hemlock Falls; most knew Skinny was harmless and that he'd been born "slow." Old man Brenner even let him sweep out the hardware store three days a week and paid him a few dollars.

I recall one August afternoon when we had been passing a football about and noticed little Amy Gillis standing beneath a large Hemlock tree with tears rolling down her freckled cheeks. We all ran to her, Skinny's long legs getting him there before the rest of us. "Why are you crying?" Skinny said, bending his long frame at the waist to look into Amy's watery eyes. Amy pointed skyward at the reaching branches. "My Bendy is stuck in the tree," she said. When we looked up, we saw her kitten perilously balanced on a large limb near the top of the tree. Skinny immediately wrapped his long arms and legs around the trunk and shimmied up toward the kitten. We craned our necks as we watched him maneuver his lean frame through the dense branches like a writhing snake until he reached the fuzzy ball. Back on the ground, he gently placed the kitten into Amy's waiting arms.

"He is okay," he said, wiping her tears away with his thumbs.

I don't know whose smile was bigger—Amy's or Skinny's? I wouldn't admit it then, but I was moved by his tenderness.

I can still see Skinny walking back to the house at the end of town where he lived with his father and thinking how lonely he must be. I never saw him smile except when he was having fun with his friends. Although nearly ten years our senior, he related better with us than with the adults. I suppose that's why folks were uncertain of him because he rarely smiled. I understand now, he was more wary of them than they were of him. He had lived in a world of misunderstanding and mistrust. But in all the years that I'd known him, he had never hurt a single living thing. His juvenile mind was incapable of hatred or anger. That's why I was surprised when McGrath revealed to me the gruesome secret he had lived with all those years.

"He's a menace to this town," McGrath said to his wife.

"He's harmless," she said.

"He wasn't so harmless when he stole from Fred Darby's store last summer."

"He took an apple from the fruit stand," she reminded him. "He thought the fruit was for the taking."

"Then why'd he run?"

"He became frightened when the police arrived."

"What about the time he was caught with his trousers open behind Mrs. Henderson's rose bush in the middle of the day?" McGrath argued.

She shot him down with, "The demands of nature."

It frustrated him that he couldn't make his wife see how much of a threat Skinny was. As a boy Skinny had been a nuisance—a broken window, a knocked over flowerpot or a gallon of spilled milk, but now that he'd become a man that nuisance became a threat, at least in McGrath's mind, a threat to every civil person in Hemlock Falls. McGrath believed it was just a matter of time before someone became a victim of Skinny's inept mindless behavior, and he couldn't make her understand that.

"Well, I see the way he looks at Becky," he said, trying to hit home.

Their sixteen-year-old daughter was attractive and coquettish and McGrath was well aware of how she looked and acted beyond her age. McGrath had skirmished with more than one young man for even looking at her with what he thought was the wrong idea. Of course, he couldn't see his daughter's provocations and it was always those "young vultures." I had seen Becky at work and knew enough to keep my distance.

"It was a Saturday night in August," McGrath began, when Becky returned home later than she should have. He had been waiting up for her and when she walked through the door with her blouse torn and her hair disheveled, he became enraged, questioning her whereabouts. Although she had told him, she would be with her best friend, Lucy Ward, he was too blind to see the obvious.

"Tell me the truth," he demanded, shaking her shoulders with his big hands.

Becky stood for a moment; more afraid of her father than of the lie she was about to tell. "It was that Skinny Bigelow," she said. "He passed me on the road as I walked home tonight and pulled me into the woods. I tried to run, but he grabbed my arm and tore my blouse." Her lips quivered as tears came to her eyes. "He touched me, daddy," she said.

Even as anger welled inside him, McGrath brought her close, kissing her forehead.

"I should have come home sooner," she whimpered. "I'm sorry."

He took a deep breath and wiped the tears of phony innocence from her eyes. "Go to bed," he said, "things will be better in the morning."

After she left the room, he stood by the front window staring out at the darkness for a long while, the hatred and anger seething within him. It was then that he'd decided to kill Skinny Bigelow.

I was surprised McGrath could entertain such an idea and found it hard to believe he would carry it out. Although he had seen action in the military and often bragged about how many "gooks" he had killed, committing murder was something different.

***

McGrath stood on the edge of the woods and watched the road from behind a large tree. He knew Skinny would leave the hardware store that evening and pass through the woods on his way home. The sun hadn't set, but the woods were dark and he could pull Skinny into the trees the same way Skinny had pulled his daughter into the trees and there he would rid himself and Hemlock Falls of this menace. When the deed was done, he would bury the body deep in the woods. He leaned on the long handle shovel he had brought with him and waited.

It was more than a while before Skinny came sauntering up the road toward Alex McGrath. He walked with his head down—singing "Old McDonald" which was the only song he knew, or could remember—and kicked at an occasional stone in the road just for fun. McGrath couldn't see Skinny's juvenile innocence, only the threat he had perceived in his own sick mind. Pressing himself against the tree, he rested the shovel on his shoulder, gripping the handle with sweaty palms.

"As he passed me," McGrath explained, "I stepped out and swung the shovel in a wide arc." He tried to demonstrate with his frail arms but they dropped quickly to his sides. Skinny, not being much of a target, turned quickly, and the shovel missed its mark. Terrified and confused, he shouted: "Why! Why!" as he ran blindly into the woods—just where McGrath wanted him.

McGrath followed close, swinging the shovel wildly as he ran. Skinny scrambled up a small embankment losing his footing more than once but rising just in time to miss the next deadly swing from the shovel. As he reached the crest of the embankment, he tumbled on a web of roots and fell to the ground. McGrath was above him quickly and brought the shovel down hard, but Skinny grabbed the long handle and held it firm.

"Why do you do this?" he cried.

McGrath yanked the shovel free as Skinny curled himself into a tight ball and buried his face in his hands. Mercilessly, McGrath brought the shovel down a second time. I cringed as he coldly detailed how the shovel struck the back of Skinny's head with a *crack* and how blood rolled out of Skinny's skull onto the cry leaves beside his now dead body. McGrath dragged the lifeless form deeper into the woods. I asked him to spare me the details of how he'd disposed of the body and he gratefully obliged. It took

The Secret of Skinny Bigelow

more than an hour for him to complete the sordid task, and it was dark when he walked—unnoticed—the two miles back home.

As McGrath unfolded more of his story, I couldn't help thinking he felt satisfied, almost proud of what he'd done. It was difficult for me to believe McGrath's confession of this cruel, calculating crime. For years the mystery of Skinny's disappearance had plagued me and now I had found out the truth. How had McGrath tortured himself in silence for so long?

The following morning, the news of Skinny's disappearance spread through Hemlock Falls. Skinny never returned home from work on Monday and Carl Bigelow went to the police to report his son missing. The police began a missing person investigation but had nowhere to go with it. McGrath remained silent and resolute in keeping his secret, seeming as shocked and bewildered as the other town residents. He read the details of the case from the evening paper to his wife and even volunteered to be part of a small search party to look for Skinny. The police hypothesis was that Skinny—being mentally challenged—had gotten himself into some kind of natural trouble or had become a victim of an accident. They had no reason to suspect foul play.

Days passed, and Skinny's disappearance remained the buzz of Hemlock Falls. The police had nothing substantial and although theories abound, no one knew for sure where Skinny was, in time interest in his disappearance waned.

McGrath said the following weekend was the beginning of his personal Hell. As he continued, I watched tears spill from his already moist eyes and travel down his cheeks. For the first time, I felt he might be showing some semblance of remorse for his actions.

While waiting up for Becky who had been making a habit of coming home later than she should have, he received a call from Sheriff Harmon of the county police. Harmon said that Becky and Lucy had been walking home when they'd decided to take a shortcut through the abandoned Mason farm to gain time. From the best he could decipher of Lucy's explanation—as Becky ran ahead passing the old farmhouse; she stumbled into a small hole in the ground, which might have been the remnant of an abandoned well. Lucy tried calling to her but received no reply. Frightened and hysterical, she ran home and her parents who notified the police. The sheriff suggested McGrath come to the farm immediately.

When McGrath and his wife arrived at the Mason farm, there were already police and rescue workers on the scene. A group of townsfolk, including myself, had gathered there out of morbid curiosity. An ambulance had its headlights directed over the area where Sheriff Harmon and the others were standing. McGrath held his wife close as they approached.

"I'm sorry, Alex," the sheriff said, stepping aside to allow them a better view. He was a tall man with a handlebar mustache and wore a wide brim Stetson hat. "Keep behind the tape," he warned, "the soil is loose."

McGrath saw several wooden stakes in the ground bound with yellow "caution" tape, encircling a dark hole in the earth. Rescue workers had rigged a droplight and lowered it into the hole. McGrath peered into the opening, which seemed only slightly more than twelve inches in diameter. As he looked deeper, the yellow light revealed a larger opening below, perhaps six feet wide and thirty feet deep. At the bottom, on the muddy earth floor, lay his daughter sprawled like a broken doll.

"Is she—?"

"She's still breathing," the sheriff said, "but unconscious."

"Why haven't you gotten her out?" McGrath's wife said.

The sheriff took them by their elbows and led them away from the area. He looked at them somberly. "We have a special problem," he said. "You can see that opening is just a bit over a foot in diameter, and the surrounding earth is as loose as sand. A heavy weight could send it all crashing into the hole, burying Becky."

"Well, how do we get to her?" McGrath said, his wife sobbing on his shoulder.

"Normally, we would lower someone into the hole but the opening is too small for anyone with enough strength to fit through and with that loose earth it's too risky. If she was conscious and we knew her physical condition, we could lower a rope, have her tie it around herself and pull her out. She could then maneuver herself through the narrow opening. You can understand we have a special circumstance here."

Several rescue workers swung a boom over the hole and began cautiously lowering a wire cable and vinyl tubing through the center of it.

"We're going to pump fresh oxygen down there to help revive her," the sheriff continued, "and a microphone so we can communicate if she regains consciousness. Right now we don't know the extent of her injuries."

"There must be some way?" McGrath said. "With all the specialized equipment these people have."

"The county has a piece of equipment," the sheriff explained, "which is a hydraulic claw-like device that is lowered and locked around a disabled victim by working levers from above. But if we were to use it and Becky has internal injuries...it could be fatal."

The sheriff wiped the perspiration from his forehead with the back of his thumb then went on. "With all this so-called special equipment, the human factor is still the best hope. We're not sure how to proceed at this point but if she stays down there much longer..."

In hysterical desperation, McGrath's wife broke away from him and rushed toward the open pit. "My little girl!" she cried. "Save my little girl!" McGrath caught up with her, wrapped his arms around her waist and pulled her back from the pit in enough time to prevent more of the loose earth from falling into the hollow. He lifted her face to his and kissed her consolingly on her forehead. He looked into her eyes, swollen now with tears, then back at the dark pit where his daughter lay dying. As his own eyes filled with tears, he was overcome by the realization that he had made an irreparable error, a rush to judgment that would cost his daughter her life and be his punishment for the rest of his days—an agony he'd have to suffer in silence.

While his sobbing wife buried her face in his chest, he continued staring into that would-be grave, helplessly awaiting a savior, silent with the thought that the only person with enough strength, who could have easily fit into that opening to save his daughter's life, was—Skinny Bigelow.

Welcome to The Doll House

Margaret Grimes looked up at the sign hanging above the door of the little shop with trepidation. Its weathered black letters announced: THE DOLL HOUSE. With a sweaty palm, she turned the brass doorknob and stepped inside. The pungent odor of cut wood and paint thinner stung her nostrils, and she discreetly pinched them together with her fingers before the man behind the counter could notice. He was a short man with a full head of silver hair and a well-cultivated mustache that drooped well beyond the corners of his mouth. He wore bib overalls over a long sleeve checkered shirt, a pair of wire-rimmed glasses rested easily on the bridge of his nose. In one hand he held the head of a doll, while he delicately ran a comb through its long black hair. He peered over his glasses as he watched Margaret shut the door and walk toward him.

"Welcome to the Doll house," he said.

Margaret removed a business card from her purse and dropped it on the counter. "I found your card under my office door this morning," she said. "I don't know who left it."

The man looked down at the card without picking it up. "A special friend is doing you a favor," he said.

"I'm not aware that I have special friends," Margaret said.

"But you have a special need," the man said, "or you wouldn't have come here." He slid the comb into the breast pocket of his overalls and carefully placed the doll head onto a wooden peg. "Come into the parlor," he said.

He walked to an arched doorway, pulled back a cloth curtain, and waited for Margaret to follow. Warily, Margaret walked through the doorway.

The parlor was a small room consisting of a round wooden table and two chairs. A workbench ran along one wall, upon which lay a variety of doll parts: arms, legs, heads and several sets of various colored eyeballs strewn about the benchtop in disarray. On the wall above the workbench hung a row of completed dolls, dangling naked by a thin wire secured about their neck, each attached to their own rusted hook as if they had been collectively consigned to the gallows.

Margaret sat at the table. The man sat opposite her.

"I was able to learn about your services through, shall we say, cryptic sources. But I'll need to know more." Margaret said.

"I conduct business with the strictest of confidence," the man said. "I need to know nothing about you, not even your name. Services are rendered to all who wish to use them and, of course, are willing to pay. All transactions are on a cash basis."

"Money is not a problem," Margaret said.

"Then," the man said. "I can guarantee complete satisfaction."

"Is it true your dolls can do anything."

"Anything humanly possible," the man said, "except procreate. I make a variety of dolls: dolls that love, dolls that hate, dolls that will do things *for* you and dolls that will do things *to* you, if you so desire. All are designed to accomplish their assigned task flawlessly."

"Are they robots?" Margaret said.

"Goodness, no. They are dolls. They possess no internal electronics."

"How then, do they do the things you claim?"

"Through a process that dates back centuries, kept secret and known only to a select few worldwide."

"Of which you are one," Margaret said.

The man smiled and continued. "My dolls have a high rate of success in achieving their assignments. They possess the ability to function as humans, but are devoid of human emotions, sentiments that might interfere with their assignment."

"Sounds like a fantasy," Margaret said.

The man smiled again. "If you'll explain exactly what it is, you need."

Margaret thought about her reasons for coming to the shop before she spoke, weighing whether she was doing the right thing.

It wasn't Daryl's unfaithfulness, or the neglect, or the verbal abuse that bothered her the most. It was the lies. The incessant lies... and the women. The secretaries in tight shirts and high heels. The women at the late-night meetings and the female associates that accompanied him on business trips. Business trips that had become pleasure trips, trips he had once taken with her.

The CEO of a large company can lose ties with his wife even after twenty years of marriage if he believes she is interfering with his career, no matter how she had stuck by him while he was climbing the corporate ladder. She had always been faithful, true to their marriage. She gave him no justification to behave the way he had. Although...there was that *one* time. An unplanned overnight with Sid Westlake from accounting. But that had been a mistake. They had both been drinking heavily and things had gone too far. And she supposed she couldn't deny the incident with Marc Rizzo. But a furtive embrace and passionate kiss on the lips was hardly being unfaithful. Besides, she had never like Rizzo and didn't know how that whole thing happened, anyway. Two minor indiscretions in twenty years was not a bad record. She felt no remorse for her imprudence. Truth was, she felt good about getting even with Daryl, giving him a dose of his own medicine. Daryl had been indifferent when he discovered what she had done, almost glad she had given him a reason to hate her as much as he believed she hated him.

She tried talking to him, but each talk turned into a heated debate, a denial, and then a shouting match. He had even slapped her face once in a burst of guilty anger, a slap that was the last straw for her, that made it easy for her to hate the man she had once loved. Eliciting that hatred now allowed her to say what she wanted without reservation.

"I want to do away with my husband," Margaret said. "I want him *exterminated, eliminated, disposed of, out of my life.*"

The man offered an amused, indulgent smile. "A colorful choice of euphemisms," he said. "What you mean is, you want your husband dead, and you wish to employ one of my dolls to kill him."

"If my understanding of your service is correct," she said.

"Your request is more popular than you'd think," the man said.

He got up and walked through a doorway behind him. A moment later he returned carrying a large rectangular box. He set the box down on the floor beside the table and removed the lid. He reached in and lifted out a doll and placed it on the floor beside him, facing Margaret. The doll stood on its own. Margaret stared at it with great curiosity. It was the representation of a young girl. It stood nearly four feet tall and was attired in a powder blue dress with white ruffles and patent leather shoes with leather bows. Its blonde hair was fashioned into twin pigtails, and its face was hand-painted with glossy colors giving it a countenance that appeared amiable, yet strangely sinister. Its lips were deep red, its cheeks shaded a vivid pink. But its eyes are what held Margaret's attention. They were large and round with limpid blue pupils that sparkled with an extraordinary realism. It seemed as though the doll could see through them.

"This is my model: K-15," the man said," a model more than adequate in performing your requested task. It comes in a variety of appearances, but I chose this one because she resembles you."

Margaret thought of her own blond hair and blue eyes but wasn't sure whether to take the man's sentiment as a compliment.

"It's beautiful," Margaret said, "much too beautiful to perform such an immoral deed."

"Quite often it's the most beautiful that are the most immoral," the man said.

"Is it able to move?" Margaret said.

"When it's required to," the man said.

"Can it talk?"

"If it needs to."

As if on cue, the doll turned its head a quarter turn, looked at the man, then turned back to look directly at Margaret. The painted lips did not move, yet Margaret heard the doll say, "My name is. K-15 and I'm here for you." in a high pitched youthful voice.

Margaret sat astonished. She hadn't seen the man put his hand anywhere on the doll; push a button, pull a string or do anything to set the doll in motion. Yet, it had turned its head and spoke directly to her.

"Amazing," Margaret said.

"Its mission is to serve you," the man said.

"But how will it—"

"When the time comes, it will know what to do."

The man lifted the doll carefully, placed it back into the box and replaced the lid.

"Have you given thought as to how you would like the incident to occur, time and location? All this information must be provided before we can proceed."

"I've thought about how I might do it if I were to do it myself," Margaret said.

"Excellent," the man said. "Tell me."

"I would do it just before I leave on a business trip," she said. "I have one scheduled for next weekend. Then I would have an alibi."

"And how exactly would you do it, by what means? There are many ways to commit murder."

"I was hoping for your suggestions," Margaret said. "But I'd want it to be quick."

"Quick is always best," the man said.

"And effectual," Margaret added. "I wouldn't want to be suspected of the crime."

"There is never a concern of being caught," the man said. "That's the beauty of the system. Would anyone suspect an inanimate object of doing such a thing? Besides," he said with a wry smile, "dolls don't have fingerprints."

He lifted the box and placed it on the table. From the workbench, he found a ball of twine and began to wrap the twine around the box as he spoke: "You will set things into motion early in the morning," he said. "Place the doll in the room with your husband just before you leave for your trip and before he awakens. See to all the necessary details I will explain. The deed will be done while you are away, therefore procuring your alibi."

"And afterward, what becomes of the doll?"

"It is yours to keep."

"I won't need it," Margaret said. "Besides it could be incriminating evidence. How would I explain it to the police?"

"What is there to explain?" the man said. "It is a doll."

Margaret smiled for the first time since she'd walked into the shop. The idea was genius. Murdering by proxy and getting away with it, simple and foolproof. Who would even remotely believe a doll could do such a thing? She wasn't sure she believed it herself. Was this black magic, voodoo, some mystical power passed down through centuries and stewarded by a select few as this man had claimed. Or was it some elaborate modern-day trickery designed to dupe a desperate, gullible victim in a "get rich quick" scheme. It didn't matter. If it worked, and she was rid of Daryl, it was worth the risk. For some strange reason, she believed what this man was telling her. If his claims were viable, her problems would be over.

She was beginning to feel better already.

"What happens now?" she said.

The man tied a large double knot in the twine and slid the box closer to Margaret.

"You take the K-15 home," he said, "and keep it out of sight until you're ready to use it."

***

It was nearly 5:00 a.m. by the time Margaret finished dressing. She had packed one piece of luggage the night before and assembled a small carry-on before she started to dress. Her flight was for 7:30. It was a twenty-minute drive to the airport. She had plenty of time to set up the doll. She looked over at the bed where Daryl was sleeping. His loud snoring assured her he wouldn't wake up for hours. He always slept late on Saturdays when he wasn't working. Unless, of course, he had a clandestine rendezvous with one of his female associates or an emergency board meeting, or whatever other creative pretexts he chose to use to deceive Margaret.

She didn't matter. After today, he'd be out of her life. He would get what was coming to him for treating her the way he did. He would no longer have his chippies, his hussies, his pseudo lovers. They would all miss him, (or his money) when he was gone. But not Margaret. She would be relieved of his burden, his lies, his infidelity, his verbal and physical abuse, and his blatant ingratitude.

She carried her luggage and carry-on across the room and set them on the floor by the bedroom door. She looked around. Everything appeared as it should. All she had to do now was retrieve the doll from the closet where she had hidden it and set it on the chair beside the dresser. The doll maker had assured her it would be as simple as that. The doll would know what to do when the time was right.

She had kept the doll in its box at the far end of the walk-in closet covered with several shoe boxes and a winter comforter She opened the lid and lifted the doll out carefully. Its eyes were open. *They were always open.* Margaret felt oddly self-conscious as the doll watched her every move. "You evil woman." it seemed to say as she carried it across the room. "You're the evil one," Margaret thought, "the deed doer." But her words offered her little comfort, knowing she was just as much a part of this sinister deed as was the doll.

She placed the doll on the corner chair facing the bed. From her coat pocket, she removed the carving knife she had gotten from the kitchen drawer earlier. It was a wide blade knife at least eight inches in length and she was sure it would accomplish the task nicely. She placed it on the chair beside the doll. The doll sat looking straight at Daryl, where he lay half covered by the satin sheets, one naked leg draped over the side of the mattress. Margaret clicked off the small lamp on the dresser, leaving the room bathed in the gray morning light entering from the windows. She walked to the bedroom door and opened it, picked up her luggage and carry-on and took one last look around the room. Daryl stirred once but continued snoring. The doll sat motionless. Satisfied, Margaret closed the door gently, then went downstairs to meet her cab.

In the quiet stillness of the room, the doll turned its smiling head toward the door, then turned back to look at Daryl.

***

The stabbing pain in his left shoulder shocked Daryl awaken from the black caverns of his sleep. He sat up, dazed and confused and unable to see clearly the thing that was standing beside his bed. When he reached across with his right hand and felt his painful shoulder. His hand came away wet with blood.

He had never had a nightmare like this. Not one so real. Not one with a monster that was trying to kill him in his bedroom.

He saw a quick flash…a knife as it came down in a wide arc above him. The blade, shiny and long, reflecting the morning sun that squeezed through the window blinds. He rolled quickly to his left, just before the blade plunged into the mattress. He sprang to his feet, rubbing his eye, frantically trying to focus on this sudden adversary.

The thing, whatever it was, turned for him again, the knife held high above its head. He could see it more clearly now as his eyes began to focus. Was this a man? A woman? It looked like a little girl. But it wasn't adorable. It wasn't cuddly. It appeared sinister. Its eyes cold, hollow and unmoving as it advanced toward him. Its face expressionless save for the sardonic grin that lifted its rosy cheeks and separated its painted red lips. What was he seeing? What horrifying specter had he evoked from the depths of his sub-conscience?

The child, the little girl, the doll, whatever it was, lashed out at him with the knife again. Holding that perpetual smile, as if it were enjoying the hunt. He jumped back, but not quick enough. The blade caught his right forearm. He cried out in pain. Blood streamed down to his wrist and fingers and spilled onto the carpet. He feinted to his left as the thing lunged at him again. He grabbed for its arm in an attempt to dislodge the knife, but the thing was quick and he lost his balance and tumbled to the floor. Before he could get to his feet, it was on him. Each time he tried to defend himself it would counter with a move that easily overtook his best efforts, moving with great efficiency as if each move had been rehearsed or programmed, as if it knew what his next move was to be.

The knife came up again, and down, missing his neck by inches. Cold, hard fingers gripped his throat and began to squeeze. He pulled and tugged and tried to pry them away, but their strength was greater than his. When would he wake up? When would this nightmare be over? How long could such an episode of terror continue?

And then he felt the fingers slip from his sweat-soaked neck. With a quick thrust, he pushed the thing off his body and sprang to his feet. Scanning the room, he scooped up a brass statuette from the dresser. He watched the thing get to its feet and without hesitation move toward him. When it was close enough, he swung the statuette as hard as he could, striking the side of its head. The head shattered like a glass globe, sending fragments of plastic and tufts of hair about the room. With pieces of its head and face missing, the thing swayed on its feet for several moments in a display of utter horror before toppling to the floor with a clatter.

Daryl sat on the edge of his bed. Out of breath and overcome by the realization that this was not a nightmare, that he was in the presence of something inhuman. His wounds were real. His pain was real. As incredible as it seemed, he had killed something in his bedroom.

He got up and walked closer to it. It looked like a young girl, a large doll, not human, but synthetic, dressed in a pretty blue dress. Its blond hair was done up in pigtails. Its head had been partially destroyed by his blow, leaving jagged pieces of skull to which tufts of hair remained affixed. One eye socket was still intact, the eyeball having rolled back into the head leaving a pure white sightless globe. Part of the chin remained and a portion of the lips, still offering the semblance of a smile. The powder blue dress was bloodstained. He was sure it was his own. This thing didn't bleed. He looked down into the skull, a void as hollow as a carved out pumpkin. Gingerly, he touched the thing's forearm. It was as cold and rigid as a corpse, a lifeless, yet living cadaver born of his worst nightmare. A spawn from Hell. Yet, it was there. He could see it. He could feel it.

He put on a pair of sweatpants and went to the bathroom. At the sink, he filled the plastic cup with cold water from the swallowed it down. He washed his injured shoulder with soap and water, applied a small gauze pad and taped it as best he could. He washed the dried blood from his forearm and wrapped that as well. He splashed cold water on his face and rubbed it through his hair, hoping it would awaken him from the nightmare he believed he was still experiencing. He hoped the thing on the floor would be gone when he returned to the bedroom. He loaded his toothbrush with toothpaste, the new spearmint flavor that Margaret insisted on buying. Although he had told her again and again, he hated spearmint.

As he brought the brush up to his mouth, he saw the thing in the mirror behind him. It was alive! The hand gripping the knife came into view. He twisted his body away just as the knife came down and clattered on the edge of the porcelain sink. He dodged passed the thing and ran back into the bedroom.

No time for the door. The thing was out of the bathroom and coming toward him, holding the knife threateningly in the air. He waited and watched as it moved with an awkward gait, limping to one side and dragging its left leg, making its presence even more eerie to behold. Its single eyeball rattled in its socket, revealing a glossy white sphere, a blue iris and then glossy white again. He backed himself against a far wall, nearly panic-stricken, waiting, watching its every move. And then, like a marionette whose strings had suddenly been cut, the thing collapsed to the floor. What was left of the head detached from its neck, and the arm and hand that held the knife separated from the torso.

Daryl stood in the silence, trying to breathe easier. He couldn't be sure the thing was dead. Or if it could be killed. He was sure now, this was not a creation of his imagination. He had his blood and wounds to prove it. But what was this thing? Why was it here and where had it come from?

Cautiously, he stepped forward for a closer look. As he did, his foot brushed against a large jagged piece of what had been a rear portion of the skull, bringing his attention to a white label that had been attached to the inside. He picked it up and read what appeared to be a manufacturer's logo in bold letters. It revealed the name and address of THE DOLL HOUSE.

***

It was well past midnight when Margaret returned home from her business trip. Her plane was delayed by several hours, much to her frustration, and she had been exceedingly anxious to discover what might have or should have, transpired during the weekend. If things went as planned, as the doll maker had assured her they would, this would be the first day of a new life for her.

She set her luggage down in the hallway and shut the front door behind her. The house was dark and silent, lit only by the silver haze of a full moon streaming through the windows. She started up the stairs to the bedrooms, not sure what to expect. She was the innocent working wife returning home from a business trip eager to see her husband after a long weekend away.

Eager to see him dead!

At the top landing, she stood alone in the saturated silence outside the bedroom door. Maybe he had left for one of his weekend "business trips". Or perhaps the doll had accomplished what she hoped it would. The silence was ominous, and she was almost afraid to enter the bedroom. Warily, she pushed back the bedroom door.

The room was dark, save for the subtle moonlight casting irregular rectangles on the carpeted floor. She closed the door behind her and looked around. The king-sized bed was unoccupied, made up tight and neat. The bathroom door was ajar, the light behind it spilling out onto the bedroom floor. She approached the door and peered through the opening. The room was empty, impeccably clean and smelled of Daryl's aftershave. Where was Daryl? She had expected to find his body strewn across the bed or lying on the bedroom floor.

She searched the remainder of the house. No Daryl. She opened the kitchen door and looked into the garage. The Jaguar was gone. *He was probably away with one of his Harlots.* She should have known he would take advantage of her absence.

She returned to the bedroom and turned on the small bed table lamp. The room appeared as it should, neat and orderly. Where was the doll? She opened the closet door. Her things were in their usual place. But no doll. She looked in Daryl's closet. No doll.

Daryl was gone and so was the doll.

She sat on the edge of the bed to collect her thoughts. She slipped off her shoes and took the ribbon from her hair. She would shower and try to get some sleep. Tomorrow she would see the doll maker, and hopefully, find an answer to what might have gone wrong. He had guaranteed success and if she hadn't gotten what she'd paid dearly for, she wanted her money back.

She was on her way to the bathroom when she heard the sound. It had come from the hallway just beyond the bedroom door, a soft sound, like the shuffling of shoes on the wooden floor. "Daryl? she whispered. No answer. Just the clicking of the door latch as she watched the doorknob turn, left then right. The door opened slowly, silently, gradually revealing an obscure figure standing in the shadows of the hallway.

Who is this, she thought, as the figure walked out of the shadows and into the soft room light? It looked like a man, short, slender, muscular. But it wasn't a man. It appeared to be a young boy, dressed in denim jeans and a long sleeve red flannel shirt. His dark hair was tousled and fell over his forehead just above his large owl-like eyes. His lips were thick and red and held in a permanent smile. In his right hand, he carried a short handle axe, which he raised in the air as he advanced closer to Margaret. The uncanniness of what she was seeing caused her to remain frozen where she stood. She wanted to scream. She wanted to run. But she could bring forth neither sound nor movement.

This wasn't a man or a boy. She could see it now in the room light. It was a boy doll! And she knew exactly where it had come from, and what it had come to do.

The Man in The Wall

The first time Bixby heard the voice, it was just after midnight. It was merely a whisper at first, low and soft and nearly discernable. But when he sat up in bed and listened harder, he was sure he could hear words. At first, he couldn't make them out, just a litany of broken sentences and phrases that didn't make sense, permeating the darkness of his room. He thought the voice might be coming from outside his window. But when he turned on the small light on his night table, climbed out of bed and stood before the window, he heard the voice coming from behind him. He was sure then; the voice was in the room with him.

He returned to his bed and sat up against the headboard, listening intently until he was sure the voice wasn't just in his head. Perhaps Aunt Effie had become ill, and he was listening to her verbal agonies brought on by a bout of nausea or a severe headache. But no…the voice was too steady, too constant, almost like someone reciting a verse or deep in prayer. He couldn't tell from which direction the voice was coming from, but he thought he heard it most clearly coming from behind the large windowless wall across the room. But his room was at the corner of the building, and there was no room on the other side of the wall. He was sure of that.

He got out of bed and walked toward the wall. When he was close enough, he reached out and touched it warily as if it might be something he should fear, something ominous, something

The Man in The Wall

that might do him harm. But it was just a wall. A wall painted a soft green designed to soothe and comfort the room's occupant into a restful night's sleep. He leaned closer and pressed his ear to the wall—and that's when the voice stopped!

He stood in the quietness of the room listening to his anxious breathing.

"Hello," he finally said aloud. "I can hear you."

There was no response from within the wall.

Feeling courageous, he tapped on the wall with his knuckles. "Are you in there?" he said. "What is it you want?"

He heard what sounded like a low moan, carrying with it all the agonies of Hell. It chilled his blood, and he stepped back a few inches, not sure what to do next.

Why was he hearing this voice? Does a normal person hear voices when there's no one there? But he was normal. He was sane. The time he had spent with Dr. Bergman had proved that. Dr. Bergman had told him so. Even though he was a man now, he was allowed to come back to his boyhood home and live once again with Aunt Effie, his mother's sister. He even had his old room back. Although it didn't look much like it had when he was a boy. Most of the furnishings had been removed, and the flowered wallpaper stripped so the walls could be repainted. But Aunt Effie had promised him that the room would be put back the way it had been when he was growing up. He wasn't sure how long he had been home. It seemed like a long time. But Aunt Effie would keep her promise and he'd wait until she was ready. At least he was sleeping in his own bed. The one he had slept in as a boy. The mattress was a bit lumpier now, and the bed seemed a bit smaller than he remembered, but he had been happy and comfortable here...until he began to hear the voice.

He moved closer to the wall again and listened, but heard nothing.

"I know you're in there," he said. "Why don't you speak to me? If you tell me what you want, perhaps I can help."

"Save me," the voice from within the wall said.

It was a man's voice. He could tell that now, being as close to the wall as he was.

"What shall I save you from?" Bixby said.

"Let me out," the man said.

"Who are you?"

He waited for an answer. It came as an inarticulate mumble of words he couldn't understand.

"How did you get in there?" Bixby said.

"She put me in here," the man answered.

"Who put you in here?"

Again the answer was muddled and undecipherable.

"You'll have to speak more clearly," Bixby said, "if you expect me to understand you."

There was an agonizing moan again from inside the wall and Bixby began to feel empathy for the man inside.

"Who did you say put you in there?" Bixby said.

"She did," was the reply.

"Who might *she* be?"

"Aunt Effie," was the quick answer.

Bixby was stunned. He couldn't believe what he had heard. Aunt Effie had always been kind to him, and he loved her dearly. How could this man say such a thing?

"Why would Aunt Effie put you in the wall?"

"To punish me."

"Punish you for what?"

Bixby heard movement in the wall as if someone were shifting their position on the other side of the partition. After a measure of silence, the man said, "I was a very troubled boy growing up. Aunt Effie had her hands full with me while I lived here with her. She tried to get me on the straight and narrow, but each punishment she imposed, I endured, and to no avail to her, until she put me inside the wall. I would stay here until I learned my lesson, she said."

"You speak of Aunt Effie as though she were your aunt," Bixby said.

The Man in The Wall

"She is," the man said. "I was sent to live with her after my mother died."

"I don't believe you," Bixby said. "Aunt Effie would never do such a thing."

But it could be true, Bixby thought. Although he loved her very much, and he knew she loved him, she had always been a harsh disciplinarian. After his mother passed, she was kind enough to let him live with her, although she had imposed more discipline on him than his mother ever had. It was okay that she kept him from making friends and socializing. She sacrificed her afternoons for him, teaching him his schooling, for which he was grateful. His friends were in his books. If she hadn't taught him to read, he could never have enjoyed *Tom Sawyer* and his other favorite books. Although he had resented her actions, she assured him it would be the best course of action for building him into a righteous man someday. She knew what was best for him.

He looked over at the empty bookshelves on the wall near his bed. His collection of books was no longer there, but he knew Aunt Effie would put them back when she rearranged his room like she'd promised.

"She took my books away, too," the man in the wall said.

"After she put you in the wall?"

"Before that," the man said. "It was an early punishment."

"Did she give them back?"

"She promised she would," the man said, "but she never did."

Aunt Effie had taken some of his favorite books from him when he had done something she didn't like. He couldn't remember which ones she never returned.

"How long have you been in there?" Bixby said.

"A long time," the man said. "I am a man now, about your age. But I was just a boy when she put me in here."

"Why hasn't she let you out?"

"I hadn't learned my lesson, she said."

Bixby thought such a lesson was beyond harsh, much worse than taking his books away. But Aunt Effie knew what was right, and it was probably for the best.

"What did you do to make Aunt Effie decide to teach you such a lesson?"

"I ran away," the man said.

"From what?"

"Aunt Effie."

"Why?"

"She can be too harsh if you let her," the man said.

"If you let her?"

"There are ways to stop her."

"But she's always been good to me," Bixby said

"Good to you?" the man said. "Has she always given you what *you* wanted or what *she* wanted?"

Bixby thought about what the man said. He had never thought of Aunt Effie in that way, and it made him uncomfortable to think that way about her now. He changed the subject quickly. "If I let you out, Aunt Effie might be upset with me," he said.

"She wouldn't know. I'd leave and she would believe I am still in here."

"How can you be sure?"

"She hasn't been to see me in a very long time. Probably forgot I'm here."

"How can I let you out?" Bixby said. "I can't tear the wall down."

"There might be an easier way," the man said. "Maybe you can ask Aunt Effie to end my punishment and release me. Then I could just leave here and she wouldn't be upset with you."

"I'm not sure I can," Bixby said.

"She loves you very much," the man said. "She'll do almost anything for you."

"But I won't see Aunt Effie until she brings me my breakfast tray in the morning."

"You can ask her then," the man said.

***

The Man in The Wall

Bixby didn't hear the man in the wall speak for the rest of that night. He sat in his bed looking out his window, watching the sunrise above the trees, as the growing light brought in the morning. His room was still, and quiet until he heard the door key turn in the lock. He sat up quickly as Aunt Effie entered the room carrying his breakfast tray. She set it at the foot of the bed, admonishing him not to knock it over while she retrieved the serving table from the hallway. She set the table in front of him and placed the tray carefully on the tabletop. Then she went back and locked the door.

Bixby could see a bowl of Oatmeal, a glass of milk and a Bran muffin.

"I don't like Bran muffins," he said, almost defiantly. "I've told you that before."

"It's good for the bowels," she said.

In the past, upon her insistence, he would eat the muffin and then lie awake all night with stomach pains. But now, no matter what she said, he wasn't going to eat it.

"You promised to bring me a croissant," he said, "with cream."

"I did dear, and I will next time."

Bixby plunged his spoon into the hot Oatmeal and began to eat while Aunt Effie looked on. She stood there in her white apron fidgeting with his door key, which was attached to a string that hung about her neck like a piece of jewelry. She always watched him eat and stayed until he was finished. It made him uncomfortable watching her standing there watching him. He hated it when she treated him like a boy. He wasn't a boy. He was a man, a man with ideas. A man with his own thoughts about what he did and did not want to do. Like not eating Bran muffins.

"Aunt Effie," he said. "When will you bring my things back to my room? You promised it would be soon."

"Things take time, dear," she said.

"But I've been here for so long."

"I'll rummage through the boxes in the basement," she said, "and see what I can find."

"You promised to do that last week."

"All in good time," she said. "Eat your muffin."

He drained his glass of milk and wiped his mouth with a napkin "I don't want it," he said.

"Eat your muffin or you'll become irregular," she said with a sudden loudness in her voice. "I know what's best for you."

"You don't have to take that," the man in the wall said.

Surprised that he was hearing from the man in the wall again, Bixby stood up quickly, knocking the tray and its contents onto the floor.

"Now look what you've done," Aunt Effie shouted. "You're going to clean it up."

"Tell her to clean it up herself," the man said.

"I can't do that," Bixby said to the man in the wall.

"Oh yes you can," Aunt Effie said.

She reached out with her short arms and grabbed him by his shirtfront, but he grabbed her wrists and held them tight. He had never seen her like this before. He had never seen the anger in her face nor heard the rage in her voice.

"You need a good lesson, is what you need," she shouted.

"That's what she said to me," the man in the wall said. "Don't let her do it to you. Stop her now or you'll wind up in a wall yourself."

"Don't do this, Aunt Effie," Bixby said as he brought his hands up around her throat.

"That's right," the man in the wall said. "You know what you have to do. What I should have done years ago."

Bixby started to cry as his hands tightened around her neck.

"I don't need a lesson," he said. "I've been a good boy."

Tears rolled down his cheeks as he watched Aunt Effie's face spasm and turn purple-red while his fingers continued steadily squeezing the life from her. She coughed once and gasped for air while her eyeballs rolled back in their sockets. Her body jerked several times before it went limp and dropped to the floor at Bixby's feet.

"I killed her," Bixby said.

"You did the right thing," the man said. "She would have put you in a wall too."

"But she was always good to me."

"Are you sorry for having killed her?" the man said.

"No," Bixby said. "She needed a lesson."

"Why do you think so?"

"She didn't keep her promises."

End

Made in the USA
Coppell, TX
07 December 2021

67366612R00098